DEAD IS A
BATTLEFIELD

OTHER BOOKS BY MARLENE PEREZ

Dead Is the New Black

Dead Is a State of Mind

Dead Is So Last Year

Dead Is Just a Rumor

Dead Is Not an Option

The Comeback

Love in the Corner Pocket

DEAD IS A BATTLEFIELD

marlene perez

G RAPHIA

Houghton Mifflin Harcourt

Boston   New York   2012

The text of this book is set in Adobe Jenson Pro.

Library of Congress Cataloging-in-Publication Data
Perez, Marlene.
Dead is a battlefield / Marlene Perez.
p. cm.
Summary: Nightshade High freshman Jessica Walsh's hope of finding normalcy
in high school is crushed when fellow students develop zombie-like crushes on a
new boy, and she learns that she is a Virago, a woman warrior who fights when
her city is in trouble.
ISBN: 978-0-547-60734-4
[1. Supernatural—Fiction. 2. Zombies—Fiction. 3. High schools—Fiction. 4.
Schools—Fiction. 5. Interpersonal relations—Fiction.] I. Title.
PZ7.P4258Dcb 2012
[Fic]—dc23
2011031489

Printed in the United States of America
DOC 10 9 8 7 6 5 4 3 2 1
4500334319

*To my favorite librarians, who always find
the right book for the right person.*

CHAPTER ONE

I took a deep breath before I pushed open the door of Slim's Diner. My best friend followed me in. The smell of frying burgers wafted through the restaurant and my stomach gurgled.

"Jessica, I don't know why you don't like this place," Eva said. "Everyone comes here."

"It's my brother's hangout," I replied. "At least, it was before he left for college. And besides, the jukebox would always play 'The Warrior' every time I came near it." If there was one description that didn't apply to me, it was the title of that old song.

We both glanced in the corner where the jukebox was. It was just a regular old jukebox now. I didn't want to admit it, but I kind of missed the random selections it used to play.

"What's the story?" Eva asked. "What happened to it?"

I shrugged. "Who knows? This is Nightshade. Anything's possible."

"I heard that Daisy Giordano trashed it."

"What? Daisy would never do that," I said. As much as I envied my next-door neighbor, I wasn't going to spread rumors about her, even though Ryan Mendez, my first crush, was in love with her.

"I heard she beat up her best friend's dad on Grad Night," Eva continued. "And burned down the Black Opal."

"That's not true," I said. "I was there." The all-ages club had burned down on Grad Night, but it hadn't been Daisy's fault. Her best friend, Samantha Devereaux, happened to be my brother's girlfriend. Sam's dad, Professor Devereaux, had been arrested for the murder of Chief Mendez. Things were complicated here in our little town of Nightshade, California.

"Well, something strange happened," Eva said. "Maybe it was like *Revenge of the Pod People*, or something. I can't believe I missed it and you won't even tell me what really happened."

I didn't want to talk about the strangeness of my brother's Grad Night. Or exactly how well my one self-defense class had worked, enabling me to kick butt. Or the weird tattoo-like mark that had mysteriously appeared on my upper arm one day. It wasn't exactly a tattoo, since it actually moved sometimes, but I didn't know what else to call the swirling black ink.

I'd managed to hide it all summer, which meant no cute camis or tiny bikinis. I'd spent my days at the beach sweltering in a cover-up instead of showing off my bod like all the other girls.

There was only one other person I knew with a mark like this. I scanned the restaurant and spotted her sitting at the counter. Flo used to be my favorite waitress, but I'd been avoiding her since Grad Night, when, among other things, I noticed (a) a similar tattoo on her arm and (b) her fighting abilities.

Flo was awesome. She had almost as big a crush on Ryan Mendez as I did. That is, until Ryan started dating Daisy and I finally realized exactly how hopeless my crush truly was.

I was finally a Nightshade freshman and I'd let go of my little fantasy about my brother's best friend. Now I just wanted to find someone who would look at me the way Ryan looked at Daisy.

Eva was still talking about the Black Opal as we sat down at a table. "They're finally reopening the place," she said. "I think we should go check it out tonight."

"I thought the fire caused too much damage for them to ever reopen." I didn't mention the explosion that started the fire.

"The owner is reopening the club right here in Nightshade," Eva said. "Remember when that enormous big-box store at the edge of town closed down a few years ago? She's relocated the club there. They've been working on it all summer. One of Bethany's crushes worked on the construction. He says it's really cool-looking now."

"How would we get there?" I asked. "My parents are taking my little sisters to some kiddie play tonight."

"Bethany is going," Eva replied. "She has a thing for the lead singer of this band that's playing there tonight. Maybe she'll give us a ride."

I wasn't holding my breath. Eva's sister, Bethany, was a junior and didn't have time for freshmen.

Flo came over to take our order. Her T-shirt read UNSUPERVISED CHILDREN WILL BE GIVEN AN ESPRESSO AND A FREE KITTEN.

We decided to split a chicken Caesar salad.

"It'll be up in a few minutes," Flo said. She hesitated a second. "Jessica, I'd like to speak to you about something before you leave."

I suppressed a groan. "Sure."

"Are you trying out for the high school soccer team?" Eva asked.

I shrugged. "I survived summer conditioning," I said. "So I guess so."

4

Eva and I talked about soccer tryouts, but my mind was on something else. When Flo set our salad down, I jumped. I was pretty sure I knew what she wanted to talk to me about, but I just wanted to forget it ever happened and go back to being a normal girl.

The restaurant got busy and Flo was the only server there. Taking the opportunity to avoid her a little longer, I hurried Eva along, trying to get her to stop talking and eat. She finally finished her meal, and I handed her some money.

"Would you mind paying the bill? I need to use the restroom," I said.

While she was paying, I slipped outside.

Flo saw me leave, but was forced to take care of a customer waving an empty cup in the air. She gave me one last look as she went to refill his coffee.

Eva spotted me outside and came out. I started walking down Main Street at a brisk pace.

"What's your hurry? I didn't even get any dessert."

"No hurry," I replied. "Hey, look at that. Nightshade is getting a new store."

There was a sign in the window that read, in flowing script,

The Look of Love — coming soon.

"The Look of Love?" Eva said. "What kind of store do you think it is?"

We pressed our faces to the window, but couldn't see anything.

"Take a flier," a boy said.

Eva whirled around to face the boy, who looked to be about our age. "What do you think you're doing, sneaking up on us like that?" she asked.

"What are you?" he taunted. "A scaredy-cat?"

He wasn't unattractive, but he looked at us like a buzzard eyeing particularly tasty roadkill. The boy wiped all expression from his face, but not before a gleam of anger showed.

"Take one," he repeated. "It's for our grand opening."

He stood there blocking our path, so I took a flier just to get him to leave.

Eva grabbed one and crumpled it into a ball before she threw it into her bag.

"Eva, he'll see you," I said.

"I don't care," she replied. "How dare he say I was scared. As if! I've seen *The Shining* five times and didn't even flinch."

I glanced back, and the boy was still watching us. I shivered and linked arms with Eva.

"I'm going back to give him a piece of my mind," Eva said. She was practically snorting fire.

"I thought you wanted to go to the Black Opal tonight," I reminded her. "Don't you need to go home and butter up Bethany?" I didn't really care one way or the other if we went, but it was better than Eva getting into a fight with a strange guy.

"You're right," she said. "I'd better hurry and catch her. I'll call you!"

We'd reached the bus stop, where she went one way and I went the other. Our houses were in the same neighborhood, so we always met at the bus stop.

The buttering up must have worked, because Eva called me a little while later. "Can you meet me at my house in fifteen minutes?" she asked. "Bethany said yes, but she'll leave without you if you're not on time."

There was no way I'd make it in time if I walked. I still had to get ready. I was wearing my old soccer shorts, footie socks, and PE T-shirt from sixth grade. "Mom, can you drop me off at Eva's?" I shouted.

Mom appeared in the kitchen doorway. "Jessica, what did I tell you about yelling?"

"Sorry," I said. "Can you drop me off at Eva's? Her sister is going to give us a ride to the Black Opal. If that's okay."

She glanced at her watch. "Yes, but you need to hurry. We have to leave soon for the play."

I ran upstairs to get changed. Sean and his girlfriend, Samantha, used to hang out at the Black Opal all the time when they were in high school, and she'd always dressed up. I didn't have a lot of clothes to choose from. Mom had promised to take me shopping for new school clothes, but she was always busy with the little ones.

I found my favorite jeans, paired them with a cute silvery silk top, and decided I'd put my makeup on at Eva's. I raced down the stairs as Mom and Dad and all my little sisters were piling into the van.

"You're giving me a ride to Eva's, remember?" I said.

"Of course," Mom said placidly. "You know it takes a long time to get everyone settled."

I sat next to Katie and put an arm around her. "Have fun tonight," I told her.

"I will," she said. "Sam is coming, too."

"Samantha is going to the play with you guys?" I asked. "You didn't tell me that, Mom."

"Would it have made a difference?" Mom replied. "Sam misses Sean."

My brother was attending college in Southern California, but his girlfriend had chosen to stay in town to go to UC Nightshade.

"No," I said. "But you could have mentioned it."

Even though Sean was gone, I couldn't seem to shake

his girlfriend, no matter how hard I tried. Samantha Devereaux had been the It Girl of Nightshade High and that hadn't changed one iota just because she'd graduated. I would be starting my freshman year in her shadow.

My number one goal was to step out of the shadows and into the spotlight.

CHAPTER TWO

Bethany answered the door at Eva's. For a minute, I didn't think she was going to let me inside.

"Hi, Bethany," I said nervously. Eva's big sister was intimidating, almost as bad as Sam when she was in a bossy mood. Usually, I didn't take it from Bethany, but we needed a ride. The Black Opal's new location was on the outskirts of town, almost to the freeway. There was no way my parents would let me walk there, especially not after dark, so I bit my tongue and smiled politely.

She kept me standing on the stoop as she inspected my outfit. "You're not wearing any makeup," she said.

I always felt like I was about to flunk some Bethany pop quiz, and her comment only confirmed it. I held up my bag. "I thought I could put it on here."

"Good," she said. "Because you're not going to be seen with me, looking like that."

As Bethany finally let me in, she said, "We're still waiting for Tiffany. So hurry up and do your face. She'll be here any minute."

Eva appeared and rescued me. "Any minute" turned out to be forty-five minutes, so I had plenty of time to finish getting ready. As soon as I was made up, Eva made us go wait in the hallway because she was worried that her sister would leave without us if we didn't.

"Maybe we should just skip it and stay home and watch a movie," I said.

"There is a Vincent Price marathon on cable," Eva said. "But I want to see the band. Come on, it's our last weekend before school starts."

"You're going to miss Vincent Price?" I said. My best friend was a huge horror buff.

"I'm recording it," she said complacently. "What are you so nervous about? You were the most popular girl in eighth grade."

"Eighth grade isn't high school," I said.

Bethany overheard us. "Jessica's right," she said with a sniff. "There are lots of girls who were popular in middle school who don't get noticed at all now." She left no doubt in my mind that she expected me to be one of those girls.

Bethany's best friend, Tiffany, finally showed up and

we took off for the club. The Black Opal was one of the few all-ages clubs in the area, so the parking lot was nearly full when we got there.

Nicholas Bone, a handsome guy with reddish-brown hair, was working the door. Tiffany and Bethany talked loudly and giggled whenever he looked anywhere near where we were standing.

"Hi, Jessica," he said when we finally reached the front of the line. Nicholas knew me because his girlfriend, Rose, was Daisy's sister — my next-door neighbors.

"Hi, Nicholas," I said. "I haven't seen you around lately."

"I've been helping to get the club reopened," he replied. His smile disappeared for a moment. Our eyes met and I knew we were both remembering why the club had had to close. The explosion, the Scourge, all of it was reflected in his eyes.

Bethany's "Aren't you going to introduce us, Jessica?" brought me back to the present.

"Oh, sorry," I said. I made the introductions.

After they giggled at Nicholas a little more, we paid the cover and went inside.

"How do you know Nicholas Bone?" Tiffany said. "He's ages older than you. He wouldn't be interested in a freshman."

"He has a girlfriend," I pointed out. "My neighbor, as

a matter of fact. That's how I know him." I was sure they already knew who Nicholas was dating, since they seemed to keep track of every single cute guy in Nightshade and the surrounding area, but maybe the reminder would get them off Nicholas's case.

"Lucky you." Bethany sighed. "I wish he had a younger brother."

I rolled my eyes at Eva. The older girls were even more boy crazy than usual. Bethany and Tiffany started texting. Probably each other.

"I heard Side Effects May Vary has a new lead singer," Eva said.

Bethany looked up from her phone. "What else did you hear?"

"That he's gorgeous," Eva replied.

Bethany and Tiffany giggled. "Understatement."

I tuned out their gossip and looked around the club. The new interior was a mind-boggling combination of vivid colors.

"It's certainly cheerful in here," I commented. The ceiling was painted sky blue, and fluffy white clouds floated above our heads.

Several murals in various stages of completion adorned the walls. Behind the stage, a bright orange painting dominated. When I looked closer, I realized it was a portrait of a woman, done in the style that Andy

Warhol made famous with his portrait of Marilyn Monroe. I wondered who the woman was.

"Now scram, midgets," Bethany said. "I see a table for two right up front."

"Can't we sit with you?" Eva asked.

"No, you most certainly cannot," Tiffany said as they trotted away.

"I don't see any of our friends," I told Eva anxiously. I recognized a few kids, but they were mostly upperclassmen. There were a lot of kids from the neighboring town, San Carlos, there, too.

"Relax," she said. "We'll run into someone we know eventually."

She spotted a group of sophomore boys and waved to them. "There's Connor and Noel. See, I told you."

"Jessica, come sit with us," Connor hollered. Connor and I had the same guitar teacher. Although he was nice enough, I didn't feel like sitting with them and listening to Noel rate burps all night. I gave a polite wave.

"There's an empty table," I said, and rushed over to it just as a petite dark-haired girl did.

She and I stopped short and stared at each other, unsure what to do next. "Do you want to sit with us?" I finally asked her.

She stared at me for a long moment. "Sure, thanks."

We took our seats.

"I'm Jessica Walsh," I said. "And this is my friend Eva."

"I'm Raven," she said.

"I'll go get us something to drink," Eva offered.

There was complete silence until Eva came back with a pitcher of soda and set it down, almost spilling it on Raven, but Raven grabbed it.

"You have very quick reflexes," I said.

She shrugged.

"Are you going to be starting Nightshade High next week?" Eva asked.

"Yes," Raven replied. "My aunt works there."

I started to ask who her aunt was, but was distracted by the sight of Flo sitting at a table nearby.

"What's she doing here?" I asked Eva, but Raven answered.

"Flo? She's dating the drummer of Side Effects May Vary, didn't you know?"

I most certainly did not know. I couldn't avoid Flo, no matter what I did.

Bethany and Tiffany came up to us, all smiles. "We've been looking all over for you guys."

"You have?"

"Of course," Bethany said. "And we're being so *rude*

to your friend. I'm Bethany Harris, Eva's older sister. And you're Raven Gray, right?"

"Right," Raven said.

Eva and I looked at each other. How did Bethany know who Raven was? She never paid attention to freshmen, except maybe to criticize them like she did to me.

"That means Dominic Gray is your brother?" Tiffany asked. She was trying to sound casual, and failing. *That* explained the sudden friendliness.

"Yes," Raven said.

"Who is Dominic Gray?" Eva whispered.

"My brother," Raven said wryly. "And also the new lead singer of Side Effects May Vary."

I was surprised to hear the band had a new singer. My brother used to go to their shows all the time and he gave me one of their recordings for my birthday. "I liked the old singer," I said. "Camille Clark has a gorgeous voice. I can't believe she quit." Then I realized how it sounded and added, "I mean, I'm sure your brother is a great singer, too."

I was pretty sure Raven was trying not to laugh at me when she said, "It's kind of a refreshing change."

"What is?"

"To meet someone who isn't nice to me just because of my brother," she said quietly. "Speaking of whom . . . It looks like they're on."

She was right. The spotlight came on and we turned our attention to the stage. There was no announcement; the band just came out and took their places.

"Hi, I'm Dominic and we're Side Effects May Vary."

I couldn't tear my eyes away from this singer. He had high cheekbones, a long thin nose, and gorgeous blue eyes that you'd notice clear across the room. Dominic's hair looked like he'd just gotten out of bed and come to the gig, but I knew enough about boys to suspect that he'd spent an hour, and a liberal amount of hair products, to get that just-right careless look.

I hated that I was reacting the same way as all the rest of the girls in Nightshade. To be honest, I was probably reacting the same way as every girl in the state along with a good portion of the boys. I sat there mesmerized until the band announced a break.

Eva leaned in so that no one else could hear. "Still like the old singer better?" she teased softly.

I cleared my throat. "He's all right," I finally managed to say.

"Who's all right?" a voice said behind me. I figured out who it was by the way Tiffany and Bethany acted like they'd been electrified.

"You, Dominic," Raven said as her brother sauntered up to our table. "Jessica here likes the old lead singer better."

"Is that so?" he asked. His skin was still glistening with sweat from being under the spotlights.

I mumbled something and then sank in my seat, utterly mortified. What was the matter with me? I was normally much more confident around guys.

Bethany and Tiffany glared at me when they didn't think Dominic was looking. I don't know what they were so upset about. I'd made an idiot of myself and insulted him. Hardly the best first impression.

"What exactly did you like about the old lead singer?" he asked.

I floundered for a minute while I tried to remember exactly what it was that I had liked about Camille. "Her voice was old-fashioned," I said. "Sort of bluesy."

Bethany and Tiffany snickered. "Side Effects May Vary isn't a blues band," Bethany said sharply.

"I know that," I said. "Her voice sounded a little sad, even when she sang happy songs. I liked it."

"I did, too," he said. He gave me a flirty little smile. "But I hope you'll like the new lead singer as much."

"We'll see," I said, suddenly confident. I sent a flirty smile right back. *This* I knew how to do. Flirting was practically my major.

"Are you going to stay until the end of the show?" he asked.

Before I could answer, a swarm of girls approached, and Dominic's attention turned to his fans.

"Look at the way they're crawling all over him," Tiffany said. "Disgraceful."

"What are we waiting for?" Bethany replied. "Let's go."

They jumped up and joined the girls gathering around Dominic.

"I didn't mean to offend your brother," I told Raven.

"Dominic? He's hard to offend," she replied. "Besides, it was worth it. You're probably the only girl he's met since we moved here who hasn't fawned all over him."

"Jessica's used to boys fawning over her," Eva piped in.

I frowned at her. "I am not."

"Are too," Eva said. She jerked her head in Connor's direction.

The band had returned to the stage, except for Dominic, who was having a hard time extricating himself from his groupies.

Finally, Flo left her table and went over to the girls. She said something I couldn't hear and they all scattered, and Dominic was able to reach the stage.

"You know, he's a good singer and all," I commented to Eva. "But I don't see what the big deal is."

I kind of did, but it was driving me nuts that Bethany and Tiffany were acting so boy crazy.

Raven overheard and gave me a knowing look. "Just wait," she said. "You haven't heard him sing a love song yet. You'll fall for him just like all the rest after that. You won't be able to help yourself."

"Ick," I said. "That doesn't sound like real love to me." I wanted someone who loves me, too. Not someone I have to put up on a pedestal and chase with a bunch of other girls.

I looked around the club and my gaze happened to settle on Daisy and Ryan, who were holding hands in a corner, oblivious to the rest of the world. "I want what they have."

Raven followed my glance. "Hmm, he's cute," she said. "But obviously crazy in love."

"That's what I want. A boy who is crazy for me."

As if reading my mind, Dominic broke into a cover of Madonna's "Crazy for You."

"That's not on the set list," Raven muttered, but I ignored her. I watched Dominic's performance and thought about how cute he was. Luckily, Side Effects May Vary didn't play any other love songs that night or I would have thrown my number onstage just like the other girls.

CHAPTER THREE

After the show, Eva and I couldn't find Bethany and Tiffany anywhere. The club emptied out, but there still was no sign of them.

"Do you think they're outside waiting for us?" I asked Eva.

"You stay here," she said. "I'll go check."

"We could give you a ride home," Raven offered.

"They wouldn't have left us," I said. But I wasn't so sure.

A male voice interrupted our conversation. "Yeah, I'm sure it was just a miscommunication," Dominic said sarcastically. "Not like you planned it or anything." What had happened to the flirty, friendly boy from before?

"Planned what?" I snapped. "Being stranded? Hardly."

"Look, girls try this stuff all the time," he said. "We'll give you a ride home, but you're sitting in the back."

"Because there isn't room in the front because your fat head is taking up all the space?" I replied. "I hate to break it to you, but I'm not trying to spend time with you. We'll get a ride home from my neighbor." If Daisy was still there, I knew that she would give Eva and me a lift. Or Nicholas, but who knew what time he'd get off work.

Dominic gave a disbelieving snort.

"Dominic!" Raven chastised him. "Don't be so rude!" She gave me an apologetic look.

"I'd rather walk," I muttered.

"Suit yourself," he said as I stalked off.

I found Eva at the front door. "Did you find them?"

"Bethany's car is gone," she said. "I can't believe they left us here."

"Call her cell," I suggested. "I'll see if I can find Daisy."

I didn't see Daisy or Ryan in the club, so I ran out, hoping to catch them in the parking lot. I got there just in time to see Ryan's car make a left turn and exit the lot.

I went back into the club, where Dominic approached me. "Look, I'm sorry," he said. "Let me give you a ride home."

"Why? So you can tell all your friends that some stupid freshmen girls wouldn't leave you alone? No thanks."

Dominic blushed. "I'm sorry," he said. "It's been a tough day."

I hesitated. I didn't see how dealing with girls throwing themselves at him could have been that tough, but at least he was apologizing. We were kind of stranded, so I was about to accept his offer.

Flo came up to us and had obviously heard our argument. "I'm going that way. I'll give Jessica and Eva a ride home," she said.

"Great," Eva said, obviously relieved to have that settled.

Although I'd been trying to avoid Flo, this was better than taking a ride home with Dominic Gray.

We walked out into the parking lot with the band, Flo, and Raven. I suppressed a snicker when I saw a group of girls standing by what was obviously Dominic's car.

"Raven, it was nice to meet you," I said. "Maybe we could hang out sometime?"

"Maybe," she said noncommittally. "I'm pretty busy."

"I'll see you in school, then," I said. I knew a blowoff when I heard one.

Eva and I piled into Flo's white van, which had a Slim's Diner sign on its side. I sat in the back seat and Eva took the front. I assumed the van would smell like old hamburgers and fried onions, but it smelled like apple pie.

Flo kissed her boyfriend goodbye and I looked away. Their happiness was something precious and private. But the view out the other side window wasn't much better. A very pretty blonde was talking to Dominic, who didn't seem to be paying attention. He looked over and saw me watching them and gave me a little wave. I turned away, embarrassed to be caught staring.

Flo finally got in the van and we left.

"Can you believe the nerve of that guy?" I fumed.

"Who?" Eva said. She had a short attention span, unless monsters or mutants were involved.

"Dominic Gray," I replied. "He flipped out on *me*, when those girls were practically drooling on him."

"Despite all the attention, he hasn't had it easy lately," Flo said.

I forgot, for a minute, to be nervous around her. "Girls were falling all over him and he was eating it up. And then he practically accused *us* of lying in order to spend a few minutes with him. As if."

"Why do you think he and Raven came here to live with Katrina Phillips?" she asked. "Because they didn't have anywhere else to go. Their dad died recently. So go a little easy on him."

"I didn't know," I said.

"Well, now you do," she replied.

I also now knew who his aunt was. Nurse Phillips, the school nurse at Nightshade High, who also happened to be the bass player in Side Effects May Vary.

When Flo dropped Eva off, she waited until she was safely in the house, then said, "Jessica, come up front."

I moved into the front seat reluctantly. Why hadn't I thought to ask her to drop me off first?

"I want to talk to you."

I had been dreading this. "About Grad Night?"

"Yes," she said. "But not just Grad Night. Other things, too. Why don't you stop by the diner tomorrow at around three?"

"I want to forget it ever happened," I said. "It was horrible."

Her face softened. "I know," she said. "But there's a way we can help stop anything like that from happening in Nightshade ever again. Just come to the diner and I will explain everything. Raven will be there as well."

My curiosity got the better of me and I nodded. "I'll be there."

"Cheer up," Flo said, and started the car again. "I'll buy you a milk shake."

I knew she'd just hunt me down if I didn't show up. And I had a feeling I didn't want that to happen.

CHAPTER FOUR

Sunday morning, Katie woke me by bouncing on my bed. "Breakfast time," she said. "Mom sent me up to tell you she needs help."

I looked at my clock and groaned. "She never lets me sleep in," I groused. Meals were always a major production at our house. Mom organized breakfast like a drill sergeant and everybody had a job to do.

After breakfast, I helped with the laundry. We always had tons of it. Sean was gone to college, but that still left me and my six younger sisters at home.

As I grabbed clothes out of the hamper in Sarah's room, I spotted one of my shirts. She was a year younger than me and almost the same size. My clothes disappeared from my closet on a regular basis. Since I hadn't been able to wear anything sleeveless lately, I didn't mind when she borrowed tank tops, but it would be annoying if she started snagging my fall clothes — the stuff with long, concealing sleeves.

After Mom and I finished the laundry, I said, "I thought I'd head to Slim's. Unless you need me for something?"

"Run along, honey," she said. "You've been such a big help."

When I got to Slim's, Raven and a girl I didn't recognize were sitting at the counter with Flo. There weren't any other customers in the place.

"Sorry I'm late," I said. I took the stool next to Raven.

"What kind of shake do you want?" Flo asked me as she got up and moved behind the counter.

"I don't really eat sweets," I said.

She frowned at me. "It's tradition."

Tradition for what? Raven and the other girl both had shakes in front of them, so I said, "I'll have a strawberry shake, thanks."

After Flo made the shake, she got out a can of whipping cream and topped it with a huge dollop of the stuff.

"That's probably my daily caloric allowance," I protested.

Flo gave me a smile. "Don't worry. You'll be burning it off."

I didn't like the sound of that.

Raven said, "Jessica, this is Andrea. Andy, Jessica." She didn't offer any other information.

Andy was a statuesque girl with curly blond hair, but

it was the tattoo on her left bicep that I really noticed. It looked just like mine.

She caught me staring. "Nice, huh?"

"I have one, too," I said.

"Me, too," Raven said.

"Are all our tattoos in the same place? Same shape?" Now I was really intrigued.

"I have a unicorn here," Andy said. She pointed to a spot on her shoulder. "And an evil eye on my hip."

"I just have the one on my upper arm," I said. "The swirly one."

"It's a whirlwind," Flo said quietly. "And we all have one of those. It's the mark of a virago. It's easier to just let people think it's a regular old tattoo."

"So you're a virago, too?" Andy asked me.

"What's a virago?"

"That's what I wanted to talk to you about," Flo said. "You all have the marks because you are all viragos, women warriors who fight when their city is in trouble."

Raven and I exchanged a look. She was clearly thinking the same thing as I was, which was that Flo was crazy. Or that it was a prank. I looked around for a camera, but there wasn't one there.

"Flo, you have a lot of tattoos," I commented. It was a stupid thing to say, but my brain was having trouble processing the information.

Andy shot me a dirty look. "You don't know anything about being a virago, do you?"

"And you do?"

"I know that you get the first tattoo as a novice and then a new one every year you are an active virago. That's why Flo has five. She'll have seven tattoos when she retires."

"How do you know so much about it?" I asked her.

She shrugged. "I've always known I was a virago. I've been on active duty for almost three years."

"Good," Flo said. "Then, you should be in tiptop condition. You can help me get Raven and Jessica into shape."

"I am in shape," I protested. "Besides, I haven't agreed to become a virago."

"You don't have to agree or disagree," Flo said. "You *are*."

"What if I don't want to fight?" Raven suddenly said.

"You don't want to fight?" Flo and Andy stared at her like she'd grown another head.

"I don't believe in it," Raven said. "I'm a pacifist."

Andy snorted. "You won't be when a vampire is trying to suck out your blood."

I shot her a curious look. "Are you from Nightshade? I haven't seen you around before."

"I just moved here. Nightshade isn't the only place where vampires live, you know," she said. "And some of them aren't nearly as friendly as the ones here."

"So you've fought before?" Raven asked.

"Lots of times," Andy replied. "We move around a lot for my dad's job. You'd be surprised at how much evil is out there."

"So that's what we do?" I turned to Flo. "We fight evil?"

She nodded. "In a sense. Whenever your town is in trouble, your tattoo will swirl. But you don't always know where the danger is coming from," she added.

"What now?" Andy asked. "I'm raring to go."

There was a shadow of doubt in Flo's eyes, but I'm not sure anyone else noticed it. "Now we start to train. And after the graduation night, Nightshade is on high alert. That means we patrol the city in teams. Every night."

As I finished my milk shake, I considered the news. It was overwhelming.

"Can I get you anything else? Flo told me you'd be training. Maybe you would like some protein," a male voice said.

"Nothing else," Flo said firmly. "We're going on a five-mile run."

"We are?" Raven asked. She didn't sound thrilled about it.

I looked around. "Where is that voice coming from?"

"It's my brother, Griffin," Flo said. "But everyone just calls him Slim."

"Florence's little joke," the voice replied.

I looked around again but still didn't see anyone. "Am I delusional? Or is this a prank?"

"No prank, I'm afraid," the voice said. "I'm invisible."

"Like Invisible Man invisible?"

"Exactly," he said.

"Close your mouth, Jessica," Flo said gently. "Haven't you lived in Nightshade long enough to notice things are a little . . . different here?"

I nodded, still speechless.

There was a slight stir in the air and then I felt someone sit down beside me. "I'm sorry I startled you," Slim said. "I know it takes getting used to."

"I'm sorry I acted lame about it," I replied.

"Time to warm up," Flo said. "Let's go to the park."

Once we got to the park, Flo made us stretch every muscle in our bodies.

Raven lay next to me on the ground and stretched out her hamstrings. "I hate to run," she complained.

"Really?" I replied. "I love it."

Andy made a point of demonstrating her flexibility by bending over backwards and walking on her hands.

"Very good, Andy," Flo said.

"I guess we know who the teacher's pet is," Raven huffed.

I sat up and did a quad stretch. "My parents will never believe me about this virago stuff."

Flo overheard me. "No, they won't," she said. "The truth of our existence is on a need-to-know basis, and right now, your parents don't need to know."

I stopped mid-stretch. "How are we going to explain going out every night?"

She shrugged. "You'll think of something."

"You want us to lie?"

Andy flipped over and landed on her feet. "It's simple," she said. "The lives of everyone in Nightshade, including your own, may depend upon your ability to keep a secret."

It didn't sound so bad when she said it like that.

Andy was obviously getting restless. "Let's go, already."

Flo led the way on our run, around the park, through the football field, and up hills. Five miles later, I was gasping and soaked with sweat. Andy was barely breathing hard.

I nudged Raven. "Get a load of superwoman."

Andy heard me. "Jealous?" she hissed.

"I expect you to get along," Flo snapped. "Andy, Jessica, you two have the first watch tonight."

"But, Flo," we both protested in unison.

"No buts," she said. "Your shift starts in an hour."

"Why me?" I wondered aloud.

Andy shot me a disgusted look. "Quit being a princess," she snarled. "It's your destiny, that's why."

"Is that true, Flo?" I asked. "Are we destined to be viragos, whether we want to be or not?"

"I can't answer that," she replied.

Can't or *won't*?

Flo was done with the subject. "Patrol for four hours, and then Raven will join me for the late shift. If your tattoos start to swirl, call me."

Why couldn't I pair up with Raven instead? Andy made it clear that she didn't think she needed anybody.

I guzzled down some water, and then Andy said, "Are you ready to go?"

"But Flo said our shift didn't start for an hour." I was longing for a hot shower.

Andy's lip curled. "Never mind," she said. "I'll start without you. You'll have to catch up."

"I'm coming," I said. "Relax."

"Relax and we're dead," she said grimly. She stalked off without looking to see if I would follow.

We walked in silence. Andy didn't say anything for almost the entire four hours. It was dark by the time we'd made the last sweep.

It was Sunday night and Nightshade's Main Street looked deserted. "Where is everybody?" Andy said.

I shrugged. "Probably the movies."

"The entire town?" She snorted in disgust.

"No," I replied, gritting my teeth. "Some people are probably having dinner at Wilder's; some people are home. It's a small town."

"That's one way of describing it," she said. Her snotty tone made me bristle, but before I could respond, there was a loud crash. It came from the direction of the new store, The Look of Love.

Andy dashed to the front door and tried it, but it was locked.

"Let's try around back," I said. I ran behind the store and into the alley. Andy followed closely behind me. We heard another crash.

"It's coming from inside the store," I said.

There was a groan, like someone was in pain. I tried to open the back door, but that was locked, too.

Andy pounded on the door until it rattled in its frame. "Hello," she said. "Are you injured? Do you need for us to call the police?"

No reply. Andy raised her fist to pound again, but I stopped her. "Give it a minute," I said.

She fidgeted while I stood and listened. The sound was gone.

"Someone could be in trouble in there," she said. She reached in her hair and pulled out a bobby pin, then she bent down and inserted the pin into the lock.

"What are you doing?" I hissed.

"Picking the lock," she said. "What's it look like?"

"Like you're going to get us in trouble," I said. "Andy, get up! Someone is coming."

She stopped but didn't seem rattled at all. Instead, she knocked on the door again, more calmly this time.

A light went on and the door opened.

"Can I help you?" It was the same boy who'd given Eva and me fliers.

"We heard a noise and thought someone needed help," Andy said.

He stared at her. "As you can see, I'm fine." But there was a trickle of blood near his nose, and a bite mark nearly covered his entire forearm.

I stared at it. It was filling with pus. What kind of teeth would make a mark that big? I'd never seen anything like it. Definitely not a vampire bite.

"You've been bitten," Andy said.

The boy glanced down. "My . . . puppy got a little too rambunctious."

Puppy? That wasn't a puppy bite. He was lying.

"But the noise?" I asked. I tried to step into the store, but he blocked the way. "And you have blood on your face."

"I was moving a box and bumped my nose. I bleed easily," he replied. "Now, if you'll excuse me, there's a lot to do before the store opening." He shut the door in our faces.

Andy and I looked at each other.

"Do you think we should tell Flo?" I asked.

She shrugged. "Tell her what? Seems like everything's fine."

Afterward, as I walked home, I thought about everything that had taken place. Why me? Why now? Those were questions that not even Flo had been able to answer.

CHAPTER FIVE

The first day of school was Thursday, which was probably to ease us back into the school year. Mom had surprised me with a quick trip to the mall, so I had a couple of new outfits to choose from. Eva and I had been on the phone for hours the night before, debating what to wear.

"Why don't you call Samantha?" she had suggested. "She can tell us the perfect first-day-of-school outfit."

Eva was my best friend, but even she didn't get why I didn't like my brother's girlfriend. I wasn't always sure, either, except that Sam had done the one thing in high school that I wanted to do. Which was being, hands-down, the most popular girl in school. And I didn't want to follow in her footsteps and be found lacking.

"She's busy with college stuff," I said.

"She would have time for you," Eva replied. I wasn't so sure. I wasn't usually that nice to Samantha. It irritated me that Katie, my littlest sister, seemed to think Samantha was some sort of goddess, just because she made cookies with her once in a while.

I would have to figure out what to wear without the Divine Devereaux's assistance. I had other things on my mind, though. Like what to do about the virago thing. What *could* I do? Flo made it sound like none of us had any choice in the matter. We were viragos and that was that. It made me feel like something had been decided without me, which I hated.

And what did being a warrior mean, anyway? It wasn't like I'd be fighting bad guys at my high school, or anything. Principal Amador would suspend me in a heartbeat for even thinking about it. I finally fell asleep still thinking about my complicated new role.

The next morning, I spent an hour trying on outfits to make my critical what-to-wear decision.

I still hadn't figured it out when Mom's "Jessica, you're going to be late!" prompted me to go with the outfit I had on: jeans that had cost me four weeks of allowance, stacked heels, and a pale green floral top.

"Can you believe we're finally here?" Eva asked me as we walked to school.

"In high school? The day was bound to come eventually."

"I guess." She surveyed my outfit critically. "I see you managed to get in touch with Samantha."

I shook my head. "Nope, I picked this out all by my-self."

Our conversation was interrupted by a car horn.

"Hi, Eva. Hi, Jessica." It was Evan Delaney, calling out from the passenger side of his mom's Volvo. "Want a ride?"

"No, thanks, Evan," I said. "We'll walk."

Evan and I had gone to a couple of middle school dances together. He was well-mannered, good-looking, and popular.

"I can't believe you turned him down," Eva said. "He's so cute."

I shrugged. "I guess so."

"What are you talking about? He's the complete package."

"Maybe," I said. My mind turned to Dominic Gray, but I blocked the thought immediately. Dominic was not the perfect guy. He couldn't be. I couldn't take all that competition.

"Leave it to Miss Popularity to find Mr. Perfect lack-ing," Eva said. There was a tiny hint of something envious in her voice and I stopped walking.

"Maybe I'm not Miss Popularity anymore," I said. "And maybe I find perfection a little boring."

"I'll take Evan off your hands," she replied with a giggle. That sour note in her voice was gone and I felt relieved. I didn't want to start my first day of high school fighting with her.

"He's all yours," I said.

Eva gave me a shrewd look. "Maybe he's easy to give up because you like someone else."

"Like who?" I asked, but Dominic's face popped into my mind again and I blushed.

"I thought so."

"Dominic Gray is cute," I admitted. "But every girl in town is interested in him."

"They're just interested in Dominic the lead singer," she scoffed. "That's not what you're interested in, is it?"

"I can't figure him out," I said. "The fact that he's in a band doesn't matter to me, but how he treats me does."

"He seemed genuinely sorry that he snapped at you," she said. "Those other girls don't matter. Not if you really like him."

"Maybe you're right," I replied.

"You know I'm right," she said. "That's what best friends are for."

I grinned at her. "You're the best best friend ever."

"It doesn't bother you, does it?" Eva asked me.

"What? You liking Evan? You'll make a cute couple,"

I said. Even if their first names were alike enough to cause massive confusion.

Wolfgang Paxton and a bunch of other sophomore boys were lounging on Nightshade High's front steps. As Eva and I walked by, a stocky boy I didn't know said something rude that I didn't quite catch. I guessed it was about me from the way the boys stared at me and snickered.

Wolfgang was the last person I would have expected to come to my defense. "Leave her alone," he said.

"Why? Do you want her for yourself?" the stocky boy asked.

"I have a girlfriend, Tim," Wolfgang replied. "I was just trying to prevent you from losing a few teeth."

The stocky guy got in his face. "From you?"

"No," Wolfgang said calmly. "She's Sean Walsh's little sister."

"He's all the way in Orange County," Tim scoffed.

I wanted to grab that Tim guy by his thick neck and show him I could take care of myself. That would mean revealing something I wasn't ready to show the world.

"Yeah, but his best friend is right here in Nightshade," Wolfgang said. "You willing to tangle with Ryan Mendez?"

Before Tim had time to reply, Eva and I ran into the building.

I couldn't find my locker combination and had to try it three times before I finally remembered I'd written it down on the back of my schedule. I had trouble finding my English class, and I only had one class with Eva. All in all, not a fantastic first day of school.

I caught myself looking for Dominic in the halls, but I didn't see him anywhere.

After my last class, Eva dragged me over to the bulletin board outside the office. "Sign up with me," she begged.

"For what?"

"Show choir. It's after school, once a week. And it won't interfere with soccer."

"I haven't even made the team yet," I pointed out.

"You will," she said. "Please sign up with me."

"I didn't know you were interested in singing," I said.

"It's a recent interest." She avoided my eyes, but I knew that look.

"Is Evan in the choir?"

She blushed and I knew I was right. She said quietly, "He's in the science club and choir. And according to the school bulletin, the science club meets the same time as HACC." HACC stood for Horror and Cinema Club.

"That was fast," I commented. She'd already memorized his schedule, which was something I'd never seen her do before. Normally, she was much more interested

in old horror movies than boys. Eva wanted to be a director someday and thought it was never too early to start.

She gave me puppy-dog eyes, and I sighed and took
the pen out of her hand. "Okay, I'll do it."

She squealed and hugged me. "Thank you, thank
you!"

I hoped I wouldn't regret it.

CHAPTER SIX

I *had to walk home alone* on Wednesday because Eva was doing some casual loitering by her new crush's locker. I'd just left school when it started to pour down rain. It was early fall, when it rarely rained, so I didn't have an umbrella or even a jacket with me. Within seconds, I was soaked.

A car pulled up alongside me. "Want a ride?" Dominic Gray was behind the wheel.

"No thanks," I replied. "Don't you have some groupie to bug?"

"But I want to bug you," he said. "C'mon, please get in." He asked with a devastating smile and I couldn't help but smile back.

"Well, it's better than drowning," I said. "But just barely."

He let out a snort of laughter. I didn't say anything as we drove, but I noticed that he seemed to know where to take me.

"How did you find out where I live?" I asked him as we turned onto my street. He parked the car in front of my house before he answered me.

"I asked Eva," he said. "She's your best friend, right?"

"She is," I said. "But why did you want to know?"

"Look, I know I acted like a jerk the other night," he said. "I wanted to tell you I was sorry. That's all. I'm not stalking you or anything."

"Apology accepted," I said, because he seemed sincere. "And thanks for the ride." For some unfathomable reason, I wanted to prolong our conversation. It couldn't be that I had noticed his bright blue eyes, could it?

"Thanks for hearing me out," he replied. "I'd love to talk more, but I'm supposed to meet Aunt Katrina and I'm late."

"I've got to go, too," I said. "Guitar lesson."

"Guitar lesson?" he asked. "When did you take that up? When you met me?"

The question seemed hostile and it dawned on me that he thought I had taken up the guitar to get closer to him.

I stared at him. "You do have a fat head, don't you?"

"I just meant — " he started to explain.

"I know what you meant," I said. "For your information, I've been playing the guitar for three years." I didn't

45

wait for a reply, but got out of the car and slammed the door, hard.

I ran up the driveway to the house. I was going to be late for my lesson and it was all Dominic's fault.

I grabbed an umbrella and my guitar case and then ran all the way to my guitar teacher's house. I *was* late and Ms. Minerva already stood at her door. "You know the rules," she said. "One minute more and I was going to cancel your session."

She was the best teacher in Nightshade and she had kids who were just waiting to snag my spot. "I'm sorry!" I said. "It won't happen again."

"Well, then, let's get started," she said. "I thought I'd teach you a new song today."

The first part of my lesson went well, but my attention drifted. I couldn't stop thinking about Dominic, which irritated me to no end.

"Jessica, pay attention!"

My fingers tangled in the chord and I broke a string.

Ms. Minerva scolded me at the end of my lesson, which only made my mood worse. I blamed that on Dominic, too. He'd been sweet when he'd apologized, but then implied that I was chasing him. I wondered who the real Dominic was. Charming nice guy or sullen rock star?

I ran into Connor as I left Ms. Minerva's house. He was coming up the walk as I was going down.

"Hi, Jessica," he said. "How was the lesson?" His brown hair was matted with rain, but he was still smiling.

Connor was a sophomore, played in the school's jazz quartet, and was one of the nicest guys I knew.

"She's in a mood, so watch out." I started to walk away, but Connor kept talking.

"There's something I've been meaning to ask you," he said.

The rain was turning my hair into a mass of frizz, but I waited for him to finish his thought. And waited.

He finally gulped it out. "Do you want to catch a movie sometime?"

"Sure," I said, still thinking about my hair and Dominic and how my day generally sucked. "Eva's been begging me to go see *Night of the Living Dead* at that theater that shows classic movies. Maybe we could all go?"

"Uh, that would be nice, but I was thinking just the two of us." He looked at me meaningfully as he said it.

I finally realized what he was getting at. "Oh!"

His smile disappeared.

"Um, I mean, I'd love to, but you'd better get inside," I said. "Or you'll be late."

His smile reappeared. "I'll call you later," he called out as he dashed up the steps.

Had I just agreed to go on a date with Connor? He was cute, but he wasn't exactly who I'd been thinking of. I banished the thought of a pair of blue eyes and an amazing voice.

The rain had turned to a light mist by the time I made it home. Eva was sitting on my front porch, wearing an oversized raincoat, with an umbrella over her head. "Jessica," she said, "I was wondering when you were going to come home. I was just about to look for you."

"Here I am."

"You won't believe what I just found out," she said. "Remember that creepy guy who tried to give us the fliers?"

"Uh-huh," I said. My mind was still on my disastrous day.

"You'll never guess who he is!"

"Who?"

"Are you even paying attention?" Eva said. "Anyway, I thought there was something familiar about him. It was bugging me until I realized I'd seen him before. On television." She said the last part very dramatically.

"Really? What show?" I asked.

"*The Terrible Tundra*," she replied.

"You loved that show," I said. *The Terrible Tundra*

was a television show that Eva and I watched when we were about eight. It featured Jeremy Terrible, a kid who lived in the Alaskan tundra with a dog and a few survival skills.

"His name is Edgar Love," Eva continued. "He and his mom just moved to Nightshade, to open a bath and body shop."

"But the guy we met had black hair," I pointed out. "The kid who played Jeremy was blond."

She shrugged. "Ever hear of hair dye?"

"I thought Jeremy was played by someone named Ed Murphy or something like that?"

"Stage name," she said. "I'm sure it's him."

I raised an eyebrow. "What makes you so sure?"

"I cornered him at school today and he finally admitted it. But he promised me not to tell anyone, so you can't say a word."

"I won't," I told her. "How did he take the news that he'd been spotted?"

"Not very well," she replied. "He's kind of a jerk. Disappointing, really."

I knew how she felt.

CHAPTER SEVEN

That Saturday, we were training at Natalie Mason's old house. Her grandmother, a rather unpleasant woman, had lived there until she died under mysterious circumstances. Then Count Vlad Dracul, a wealthy vampire, had lived there until he and his bride went on a long honeymoon in Europe. When they got back, they'd moved into a bigger place, so the house was empty again. Natalie had loaned it to Flo for virago practice.

The flower beds in front of the house were full of huge roses. Natalie had a garden in the back, and right now, it was full of pumpkins and squash. Thanks to the green thumb of Natalie's grandmother, there were also tall privacy hedges in the back, making it a good place to learn how to fight evil in secret. I went in through the back door, which was unlocked.

I was surprised to hear the sounds of guitars tuning up. "Hello?" I called. I stopped in the doorway of the living room and saw the members of Side Effects May Vary setting up their instruments.

"Hi, Jessica," said Dominic.

Because he was rude to me when I last saw him, I ignored his greeting. "What's going on? Where are Flo and Raven and Andy?"

"They're in the basement," said Flo's boyfriend, Vinnie, from behind his drum kit. "Natalie's letting us practice here, too. Isn't it awesome?"

I nodded, and then glared at Dominic as I turned and headed for the basement. So much for top-secret fighting-evil lessons.

When I got downstairs, everyone else had already started training.

"Sorry I'm late," I muttered, but Flo wasn't paying me any attention because she was busy watching Andy showing off.

"Good, Andy," Flo said as Andy kicked a pumpkin off a dummy.

I joined Raven, who was still warming up on the mat.

"What's the lesson today?" I asked.

"From what I can tell, it's how to kill a zombie," she said.

"Zombies? Really? You've been hanging out with Eva too much," I replied.

Flo overheard me. "Zombies exist, Jessica," she said. "And you'd better realize that before you're up against one. A zombie can suck out your brains before you have time to blink."

She threw an enormous squash at me and I lashed out reflexively.

"Good," she said. "Now try it again."

I hit five squishy squash and then Flo sent me to work on strength training with Raven while Andy the wonder child showed Flo some complicated Brazilian fighting technique.

As we were working out, I heard a knocking on the door upstairs. "Do you hear that, too?" I asked Raven. She nodded.

Flo sighed in annoyance. "Why doesn't someone in the band answer that?"

"They probably can't hear it over the sound of their music," Raven said.

Since nobody else was stepping up, I volunteered. "I'll get it." It would be nice to have a break. I scampered up the stairs before Flo could stop me.

I didn't even stop to think about my sweaty, flushed appearance until I opened the back door and came face-to-face with a goddesslike blond girl with stunning green eyes.

"Hi," I said, out of breath.

She held out a hand and smiled. "Selena Silver-tongue," she said.

I shook her hand. "Jessica Walsh," I said. Then something struck me. "Are you related to the chef Circe Silvertongue?"

"She's my aunt," Selena replied. "I moved in with her right before school started." Everyone knew about temperamental celebrity chef Circe Silvertongue, but she wasn't exactly popular in Nightshade. Selena might have a hard time of it.

"Can I come in?" Selena asked. "I heard the band practicing and I brought cookies."

"Oh, sure," I said, gesturing for her to come inside. "Do you live close by?"

"Right across the street," Selena said. "Aunt Circe and the Count like this neighborhood. They didn't want to move far." She was craning her neck to see into the living room.

"Well, I better get back downstairs," I said. She gave me a smile and I felt bad that I might have judged her solely by what I'd heard about her aunt. Selena seemed nice enough, for a gorgeous blonde who apparently liked the same guy I had a crush on.

Everyone must have had blondes on the brain, because when I got back to the basement, Andy was saying, "Viragos are statistically thirty percent more likely to be a blonde than a redhead."

I glared at her. "That's because there aren't that many *real* redheads in the world," I said. "Statistically. But there are plenty of bottle blondes." I stared at her hair meaningfully and Raven let out a giggle, which she quickly stifled.

Andy was getting on my nerves. She acted like she knew everything there was to know about being a virago.

Suddenly, I felt the same strange tingly sensation on my arm I'd felt on Sean's Grad Night.

I looked over at Raven, who had a still expression, like she was listening to something or someone no one else could hear.

"Let's go!" Andy barked.

"Where do you suggest we go?" Raven asked.

"Don't you newbies know anything?" Andy said.

Flo didn't say anything but watched us closely.

"The heart of the city," Raven said.

Andy snorted, but when we all piled into Flo's van, we headed straight for Main Street. On our way out the door, we passed Selena and Dominic eating cookies at the kitchen table. I tried to suppress my jealousy and focus on the task at hand.

"Looks quiet," Raven commented from the front seat as we cruised down Main Street.

"My tattoo is still all tingly," I said.

Just then we saw a mob of teenage girls headed toward us at a run.

We were out of the van in a shot. Andy took a fighting stance, arms up, fists clenched, and I tried to copy her. Raven, I noticed, hid behind Flo.

But the mob of girls ran right past us and in the direction of The Look of Love store. I spotted Eva in the crowd and ran after her.

"What's going on?" I asked.

"It's the grand opening of The Look of Love," she panted.

"All this is because a store is opening?" I stopped in my tracks. I had thought someone was in danger, but the only danger I faced was getting sprayed with a strong perfume.

The girls were thwarted by the still-locked doors.

"Let us in, let us in, let us in," they chanted.

I stayed near Eva while the rest of the viragos fanned out and blended in with the crowd. "Why are you so excited about it?" I asked. "I thought you didn't even like Edgar."

Eva looked at me like I was insane. "Of course I like

Edgar," she said. "He handed out a ton of free samples and now everyone is dying to buy some of the limited edition perfume and body wash. Wasn't that generous of him?"

I thought she liked Evan, but the gleam in her eyes told me something else. "Huh?" was my brilliant response.

Through the glass double doors, we could see a woman clad in what looked like a purple cape. The crowd let out a cheer as she unlocked the doors. Eva and I were propelled into the store by the eager shoppers behind us.

"That must be Ms. Love," Eva said. "Edgar's mom. I can see where he gets his good looks."

I was still too stunned by Eva's complete turnaround about Edgar to respond properly.

Once inside, the shoppers fanned out. They were clearly on the hunt for something specific, and here and there, someone let out a cry of victory.

Andy and Raven came up to us, and Flo stood a distance away, observing the crowd with a faint frown on her face.

"False alarm," Andy said to me when Eva was distracted by a particularly pretty display.

"You think?" I asked. My arm was still tingling, but I couldn't figure out how a shopping frenzy was dangerous, except to the wallet.

"We're bailing," Andy said firmly. "Are you coming?"

"I think I'll stick around a little longer," I told her.

She shrugged. "Suit yourself. We're out of here."

She went over to Flo, who immediately looked my way. Andy was probably telling her I was trying to shirk the remainder of the day's training or something.

As they passed us on their way out, Flo leaned in and said, "Be careful, Jessica."

I felt a tiny bit better about my decision to stay. The store was set up so that the register was at the very back. There was an antique birdcage next to a huge potted plant near the register, and to the right, a set of black velvet curtains. I was pretty sure the curtains concealed the stockroom, since several staff members wearing purple smocks went in and out.

"I found it!" Eva crowed. "I found the last bottle of the special limited edition perfume. There were only thirteen bottles made and I found number thirteen!"

She held up a silver and black glass perfume bottle. It wasn't until she held it sideways that I noticed its unusual shape.

"It's shaped like a bird," I observed.

"It's a raven with a little silver beak. Isn't it cute?"

"What's it smell like?" I asked.

She held up her wrist for me to smell. It was intoxicating, but I couldn't put my finger on one of the subtle scents. My tattoo throbbed as I sniffed.

A long black limo pulled up in front of the store and a couple of staff members rolled out a purple carpet.

Eva clutched my arm. "He's here," she breathed, then rushed toward the doors.

Several customers whipped out cameras in readiness. Then Edgar exited the limo, wearing a white dinner jacket, black trousers, and a snowy shirt paired with a purple tie.

"He looks like he's going to the prom," I muttered.

Girls started shrieking, and what seemed like a hundred flashes went off as Edgar posed for the cameras.

"Edgar, darling." Ms. Love swept up to him and kissed his cheek.

I'd been dying to get a look in the back room and it seemed like a perfect time, since everyone's attention was on Edgar and his mom.

I drew back the curtains and started to slip in when I heard a loud "Nevermore!" It seemed to come from the birdcage.

Ms. Love rushed up. "That area is off-limits," she said, and glared at me suspiciously.

"Oh, sorry," I said in my sweetest voice.

"Nevermore," the bird croaked again, and Ms. Love drew the cover off of the cage.

"Did she scare you, my love?" She put a hand into the cage and stroked the bird's glossy feathers. He tried to snap at her, but she gave him a swift tap on the beak with her finger. "Naughty boy."

The bird glared at me with the same malevolent expression as its owner.

"Is that a crow?" I asked.

The bird ruffled his feathers, as if my question offended him.

"Poe is a raven," Ms. Love boasted. "Not a common crow."

I got the feeling she thought I'd insulted her pet.

Eva approached us. "The store is amazing." She beamed at Ms. Love.

Shannon Miller came up to us. "Did either of you find a bottle?" she asked. She brandished hers high like a trophy.

"I did," Eva squealed.

I happened to glance at Ms. Love and caught her with a triumphant smile on her face.

"I'm sorry you weren't one of the lucky ones," Ms. Love said to me in a pseudo-sympathetic way.

"Jessica doesn't need any help in the romance department," Shannon said.

"I don't?"

"She's got a thing with Dominic Gray," Eva said pointedly.

I gave her a confused look.

"What's up with you two, anyway?" Shannon asked.

"Nothing," I replied.

"Oh yeah?" said Eva. "But it just so happens you're hanging out with his sister at his band practice?"

"It's not what you think — " I started, but Eva cut me off.

"Please, Jess," she said. "I called your house to see if you wanted to come here with me, and your mom told me that's what you were doing today."

It was true that I had told my mom that. I couldn't exactly tell her the truth about virago training.

"I can't believe you're blowing off your best friend to chase a guy."

Shannon was clearly uncomfortable listening to Eva and me bickering. "I can't wait a minute longer to put some of this on."

She sprayed the perfume on her wrists and I caught another whiff. Definitely not my kind of scent.

I finally managed to drag Eva away, but she talked about the store all the way home.

"Wasn't that store cool? And Ms. Love is so stylish. I

can't believe I got one of the limited-edition bottles. Everyone is going to be so jealous of me for a change."

It went on and on. My best friend had found a new obsession, but I definitely preferred her obsession with Vincent Price movies to this one.

CHAPTER EIGHT

I had soccer tryouts after school on Wednesday. I was fairly confident I had a good shot at making the team. I'd been in decent condition before Flo's grueling workouts, but now I was in the best shape of my life.

Mr. Hogart kept me after class to talk about Open House, which I'd volunteered to help with, so I was almost late for practice. I changed in an empty locker room, then jogged onto the field to join the rest of the prospective team.

I spotted Eva standing next to Shannon and Ramona and joined them. Coach put us through warm-ups and then said, "Okay, is that everyone? We're going to start with a little scrimmage, so count off."

The scrimmage started out normally enough.

Eva and Ramona ended up on the same team, and I ended up with Shannon.

Shannon was one of those players, the special ones.

She made me play better just by being on my team. On the field, she was faster, smarter, better than anyone else, but was always kind, even when a teammate screwed up — even me. I decided to try some fancy footwork to impress the coach and fake out Eva. Instead, she didn't blink before she took the ball away from me. She left me facedown on the field, eating a nice dirt and grass sandwich.

Shannon gave me a hand to help me up.

"Nice try, Walsh," she said. "But next time, remember the basics."

Eva played defense and I was a middy, which meant I played both sides of the field, offense and defense as needed. I was getting faster. I'd even outrun Andy at the previous night's training session.

I was almost to the goal when Eva clutched her stomach and fell to her knees. I motioned for a time-out and raced over to her. "Are you okay?"

"I'm so hungry," she said. Her skin had a sickly green cast to it.

I helped her to her feet. "Why don't you sit this one out? I have a protein bar in my backpack."

The rest of the team gathered around her. Ramona handed her a Gatorade.

"I'm fine, you guys," Eva protested.

"Drink it, anyway," Coach ordered.

Eva chugged the cold beverage, and after a few minutes, her coloring returned to normal and Coach McGill allowed her back in the game.

The coach put us through the wringer during tryouts. She would occasionally scribble something down on the paper on her clipboard or shout out a command, but for the most part, she just let us do our thing as long as we worked hard.

Just when my shins were starting to scream in protest, she blew her whistle. "Good job, everyone!"

We huddled together on the field while she told us what to expect next. "First cuts will be posted on Monday."

I limped off the field, every muscle in my body sore.

Eva and I were the last ones in the locker room. She wasn't her usual talkative self, but I put that down to nerves.

I turned my back on her for just a second. I heard her groan, "So hungry," and then she was on me. She wrapped an arm around my windpipe and started to squeeze.

"Eva, quit kidding around," I said. I tried to twist away from her, but she was too strong.

I jabbed my elbow into her stomach, hard, and she released me. "Cut it out."

She stood there, looking dazed. The green color was back and a long string of drool hung off her lips.

"Gross," I said. I handed her a towel. "Wipe off your lip."

She stared at me like she didn't comprehend. Finally, she stirred and said, "What happened?"

"Did you black out or something?" I asked. "I didn't mean to hit you that hard."

"I've got to go," she said. Then she grabbed her gym bag and ran.

I stared after her, completely perplexed. My tattoo had been tingling. Was I really in danger from my best friend?

I was thinking about what could be wrong with Eva when I bumped into Connor outside of the locker room.

He was wearing shorts and shin guards. He must have had soccer practice, too. He looked worn out, but he perked up when he spotted me. "Hey, Jessica," he said.

"Hi, Connor." The last time I had really spoken to him was when he had asked me out at guitar lessons the week before.

"I called you on Saturday," he said. "Wanted to see if you wanted to catch a movie."

"Yeah, sorry, my little sister didn't get me the message until too late." I felt bad fibbing, but I didn't want to hurt Connor's feelings. The truth was, I was too depressed about Dominic and Selena to go out that night.

But I was definitely getting over it. Who needed Dominic Gray, anyway?

"That's okay," said Connor. "Maybe we can go out this weekend instead. I was thinking the Black Opal? Side Effects May Vary is playing. I know you like them."

"Sure," I said, trying to be nonchalant about it even though my heart was pounding just thinking about seeing Dominic perform again. Connor and I chatted a little more before parting ways. I smiled all the way home. I had a date.

On our date night, the Black Opal was packed. Connor and I joined Raven and Andy at a table at the front.

Flo came over to say hello, and then excused herself, saying, "I'm going to go hang out with the band. Vinnie gets stage fright."

I read her T-shirt. This one was printed with the Cheshire Cat from *Alice in Wonderland*. It read WE'RE ALL MAD HERE.

I saw Slim and his fiancée, Natalie, enter the club. I waved to them to join us, but Natalie signaled that they wanted to stay in the back. Slim wore a big cowboy hat pulled down low, a red bandanna over his chin, a blue jean jacket with the collar up, along with blue jeans and a plaid shirt. I bet he owned more trench coats than the Invisible Man.

Selena Silvertongue approached our table. "Hi, Andy," she said. "Do you mind if I sit with you guys?"

"You're welcome to," Andy said. I wasn't aware that Andy and Selena were friends, but they were both juniors, so it would make sense that they knew each other.

The band came on and Dominic gave a little wave in our direction. My heart went *thump*. I could have sworn he was waving at me, but that couldn't be true. He had to be waving at Selena, right?

"Boy, does he have it bad," Raven teased.

I could feel myself blushing. Connor looked at me curiously, but I pretended I didn't see the question in his eyes. Fortunately, the band went into the intro of their opening song and I was off the hook.

They were halfway through the first set when it happened.

"Raven, something's wrong," I said. "Look at his eyes."

Dominic's eyes were rolling back in his head.

He started singing "I'm Not Calling You a Liar," by Florence and the Machine. The rest of the band tried to keep up, but the guitarist, Jeff Cool, a stocky blond who wore way too much jewelry, had a frown on his face the entire time.

"Oh, no, not again," Raven said.

What did she mean? "This has happened before?" I asked, but she didn't answer me.

When the song ended, the band took a break, and Connor left the table to say hi to Noel.

"So how long has your brother been a seer?" Selena asked abruptly.

"What did you say?" Raven responded.

"Your brother," she repeated. "He's a seer. Didn't you know?"

"What's a seer?" I asked her.

"You live in Nightshade and you don't know what a seer is?" Selena asked. "You know, an oracle."

"Someone who predicts the future?"

Selena nodded. "Dominic just made a prediction through song," she said.

"He doesn't know how to control it and the band is getting ticked off," Raven told her.

"I can help him," Selena said. "My aunt is a very well-known sorceress and she says I've inherited her abilities."

It wasn't any of my business, but I couldn't help asking her, "If you're a sorceress and he's a seer, how can you help him? Aren't they completely different powers?"

"Are there any other seers in Nightshade?" Selena snapped out the question.

Raven looked at me and I shrugged. "Not that I know of."

68

It occurred to me that my neighbors were all psychics. Daisy or Rose or even their sister Poppy might be able to help Dominic, but they were all in college and probably busy.

"I'll talk to Dominic," Raven promised. They exchanged numbers.

Selena turned to chat with Andy, and I whispered to Raven, "I thought she and Dominic were dating. Doesn't he already have her number?"

Raven gave me an odd look. "Dating?" she said. "No, she's just one of his many admirers."

"Oh!" I said. Relief washed over me.

Connor came back to the table and rubbed my shoulder. I smiled, but I felt guilty crushing on another guy right in front of him. The band started to play again, and for the rest of the set, Dominic stuck to the set list, much to the visible relief of the rest of the band members.

Afterward, Dominic, his aunt Katrina, Flo, and Vinnie came and sat at our table. Raven made the introductions, and I watched jealously to see what Dominic's reaction would be to the gorgeous Selena Silvertongue, but he just said a polite hello.

"Selena thinks she can help you with your . . . singing," I heard Raven say in a low voice.

"How?" he asked, not bothering to keep his voice down.

"I'll explain it later," Raven whispered.

Andy yawned and stretched. "Are you guys ready to go?" she asked Raven and Selena.

"I should get home, too," Connor said. "Do you mind, Jessica?"

I stood. "Not at all." I forced myself not to glance in Dominic's direction.

On the way home, I ran out of things to talk about to Connor.

He cleared his throat. "Do you know much about Selena Silvertongue?"

I gave him a sharp look. "Not much," I said. "Why?" Was Connor going to fall for her good looks, too?

"Just making conversation," he said mildly.

"It would be perfectly all right if you were interested in her," I said. "I mean . . ." I floundered, not knowing how to say it without sounding conceited or hurting his feelings. "I think it's a good thing to date more than one person."

"Don't you think you know when you meet the right person?" Connor asked.

"Maybe," I said. "Or maybe there's more than one right person out there."

"Doesn't sound very romantic to me," he replied.

I shrugged. "I guess I'm not very romantic." But secretly, I thought I might be, for the right guy.

At my door, Connor and I did a quick awkward goodbye dance. I thought he was trying to kiss me, so I jumped away, but he was only trying to open the door for me.

"Sorry," I said. "It's just . . ."

"No worries," Connor said. "I had fun tonight. I hope we can do it again sometime."

"Yeah, me, too," I said, but my mind was on Dominic instead of the guy in front of me.

"Why don't you call me to set something up?" Connor said. There was a strange note in his voice, but I didn't pay attention. Not then, anyway.

"Sure," I said.

CHAPTER NINE

When I walked into the cafeteria on Monday, Eva wasn't at our usual table. I took my lunch tray to our spot, but I felt weird sitting all by myself. I scanned the crowd for someone, anyone I knew well enough to sit with, but fortunately, Raven plunked down beside me.

"You don't mind, do you?" she asked.

"Mind what?"

Dominic slid into the space on my other side. "If we sit with you."

"Dom's fans never leave him alone long enough to eat," Raven said.

"It's fine," I said. "I could use the company. I felt like a pariah all by myself." I threw a sideways glance at Dominic to see if he'd noticed. I had an excellent vocabulary. Better than a lot of those junior girls who'd been hanging all over him a few minutes ago. He was staring at his Tater Tots, like they held the answer to all his questions, and didn't seem to notice my showing off.

"Where's Eva?" Raven asked.

"I don't know," I said. "I saw her after third period and she didn't say anything about skipping lunch."

"There she is," Dominic said. So he *had* been paying attention. He pointed to Edgar Love's table. Every single girl at his table wore purple tops and black pants. Edgar was a stark contrast, dressed all in white.

"What's with the color coordination?" I asked. Had Eva been wearing that outfit earlier? She did look good in purple, but I couldn't help thinking that the girls were walking, talking advertisements for Edgar's mom's store, especially when they all stood and I could see The Look of Love logo on the front of Shannon's shirt.

They all left the table and put away their trays. I saw a flash of something red on the palm of Shannon's hand, but she turned and I didn't get a good look at whatever it was.

"They even walk the same way," Dominic said. "What are they, clones?"

I started to tell him about when doppelgangers had invaded Nightshade, but decided to keep quiet. I wasn't supposed to know about that, but I'd overheard Samantha and Sean talking. Besides, I didn't want him to think I was a lunatic.

Eva didn't even look my way as they exited the cafete-

73

ria. I tried not to show that I was hurt, but Raven picked up on it. "She's just excited to be in a new group," she said.

"She blew me off," I said. "We've been friends since third grade, when she moved to Nightshade. We've always done everything together."

"Things change," Raven said softly.

I stared after my best friend. "They sure do, but that doesn't mean I have to like it."

New group or not, Eva wasn't acting like herself.

"I forgot, Jessica," she said after school, when I cornered her about ditching me at lunch. "It's no big deal."

"What was with the matching outfits?" I asked.

She giggled. "It was Edgar's idea."

"Edgar seems full of it," I said.

"What did you say?" she asked.

"That Edgar seems full of ideas," I said innocently.

She nodded. "He's so creative."

I suppressed the urge to roll my eyes. She had it bad. I didn't understand what had made her switch from Evan to Edgar.

While we were talking, Edgar deigned to join us and Eva went hyper. "Jessica, I believe you know Edgar Love."

"I think we have English together," I said. I stuck out my hand, which he kissed. *Ick.*

He gave me a long look. "She'll do," he said to Eva.

"I'll do . . . what?" I said.

"One of the thirteen is out of town this weekend and we need a stand-in," Eva said. "And Edgar has approved you."

I opened my mouth to tell Edgar where he could stick his approval, but Dominic strode up and put his hand on my shoulder. "Hey," he said. "I've been looking for you."

That wiped the smirk off Edgar's face. I was having a hard time concentrating, though. The touch of Dominic's hand was doing weird things to me. You know how your stomach feels when you ride a roller coaster? His hand in mine created that same thrilling yet scary feeling.

"What about this weekend?" Eva persisted. She didn't seem the least bit curious about why Dominic had been looking for me. In fact, she ignored him completely.

"What exactly are you asking me to do?" Both Eva and Edgar seemed to think that Edgar had given me some huge honor.

"As I said, Shannon is unable to accompany us this Saturday, so Eva suggested that you would be a suitable substitute."

Could Edgar get any more pompous?

"Substitute for what?" Dominic asked.

Edgar waved his hand dismissively. "A Look of Love special event. It's essential that we have thirteen girls."

"I'm not going to be able to make it," I said.

"You didn't even ask when it was," Eva pointed out, correctly enough.

"It is Saturday afternoon," Edgar said.

"We're going to Nightshade's fall festival," Dominic said. "It's all day."

Edgar frowned. "Shannon will just have to rearrange her schedule," he told Eva, and then strode off without another word. She trotted after him.

"Thanks," I said. "I didn't know what to say to him. He gives me the creeps."

"It is weird how they follow him around like that," he said. "So what time should I pick you up on Saturday?"

My mind was on my best friend's strange behavior, so I wasn't sure I'd heard him clearly. "What did you say?"

"The Nightshade festival," he said. "I wanted to know if you would like to come with me. I was already on my way over here to ask you, when I saw Edgar."

"Really? You mean like a date?"

"Really," he replied. "And I don't mean *like* a date, I mean a date."

"Then I'd love to go," I said.

"Great," he said. He hesitated and then added, "What about that guy you were with at the Black Opal the other night? It looked like you were on a date."

I had forgotten all about Connor. "We were," I said

truthfully. "But we aren't a couple or anything." I was only a freshman, which was way too early to get serious with anybody.

Dominic and I stood there smiling at each other. The thing with Selena must have been all in my imagination. He didn't like her. He liked me. Right?

CHAPTER TEN

Saturday started out promisingly enough. I was going on my first date with Dominic and got up early, so I had plenty of time to prepare. Virago training was canceled for the day, but Flo had still made us run in the park that morning, to keep in shape.

I was ready almost half an hour early, so I went to the kitchen.

"Where is everyone?" I asked Mom. I was relieved that the house was relatively deserted.

"Katie's on a play date and the rest of your sisters went with your dad to the mall," she replied. "So what time is he coming over?"

"Two, but he's not going to want to be grilled," I answered.

To my surprise, she didn't even insist on meeting him first. "I'll wait to see if there's a second date," Mom said. "Besides, I've already met him. I sold his aunt a house about a month ago."

"You never mentioned it," I said.

She smiled. "I know." She handed me a container. "Take some cookies. Boys like cookies."

Our doorbell rang and I went to answer it.

"And don't forget a jacket. It'll get cold at night," Mom called after me.

But it wasn't Dominic standing there. It was Poppy Giordano. "Hi, Jessica," she said. "Is your mom here? I wanted to talk to her for a few minutes, if she's available."

"Come on in, Poppy," I said. "Mom, it's for you!" I called as I ushered Poppy into Mom's office.

Mom shut the door with a breezy "Have fun, Jessica."

I looked at my watch. Dominic was over an hour late. It looked like there wouldn't be a first date, let alone a second. Maybe something had happened. I tried his cell phone, but there was no answer.

The door to Mom's office opened. Poppy and my mom stepped out. "Thank you, Mrs. Walsh. I'll see you tomorrow."

"Looking forward to it," Mom replied. Then she noticed me. "You're still here?"

I scowled at her. "Yes."

"Jessica was supposed to have a big date," Mom confided to Poppy.

"Mom!" I said. "You don't have to tell the whole world I've been stood up."

Poppy smiled sympathetically. "My prom date vanished in the middle of prom," she said. "But he couldn't help it."

"Really?" Her words shouldn't have made me feel better, but they did.

"It's okay," she said kindly. She leaned in and said in a whisper, "Don't let a guy ruin your day. Go out and have fun."

I smiled at her. "Maybe I will."

Mom interrupted. "Poppy is going to be working with me," she said. "Kind of like a nanny slash personal assistant."

"You are?"

"I needed something flexible and part-time, and you need help . . . I mean, your family needs help," Poppy said. "It's a win-win."

"I guess so," I said.

"I know so," Mom said cheerfully.

Poppy leaned in. "I thought you might have something better to do with your time."

My mouth dropped open. Did Poppy know I was a virago?

She winked at me before she left.

I paced in the hallway. What should I do? I'd never been stood up before.

Finally, I decided. The festival was in the park. I could walk there. There was no way I was going to let Dominic Gray get the best of me.

It was a beautiful autumn day and it was already in the eighties. Besides, I was so mad that I was hot and sweating, so I didn't think I would have to worry about getting cold. I took a jacket, anyway.

A few blocks from the festival, someone honked at me. I turned around and saw a car pulling over and an arm waving wildly.

"Jessica, do you want a ride?" Connor was in the back seat of an older-model sedan. Noel was driving and Harmony Clare sat next to him.

I hesitated for a moment, but then nodded. "I'm headed to the festival," I said.

"We're going there, too," Connor said. "C'mon, get in."

I hopped in. At least someone wanted my company. I expected Noel to clown around while driving, but he was a serious driver and kept his eyes firmly on the road.

"I packed a picnic," Connor finally said.

I held up one of my mom's Tupperware containers. "My mom made cookies."

"I love cookies," he said.

I sent a silent thank you to my mother.

We hit traffic a few blocks from the park, then sat for many minutes before the cars started to creep along again.

"Is all this just because of the festival?" I wondered aloud.

My question was answered when an emergency vehicle raced by with its siren blaring. My tattoo started to tingle. There wasn't much I could do from the car, but I did send a text to the rest of the viragos.

Be there soon, was the terse reply from Flo.

We finally pulled into a parking spot.

When we reached the entrance, Connor insisted on buying my ticket, and then security checked my purse and patted us down.

"What's going on in there?" Connor asked one of the security people.

"Something about a bunch of girls," a tall, rake-thin guy in a Stones concert T and ragged jeans answered before the security person could speak.

There was a sick feeling in my stomach. "'A bunch of girls'?" I repeated.

"Yeah, I think they drank the Kool-Aid," he said.

"What are you talking about?" Connor asked.

"You know, they're in a cult, or something," the guy said. "They're all dressed alike and everything."

Connor and I looked at each other and then I broke into a run.

They were easy to spot — a bunch of my classmates, lying on the ground, wearing purple again. This time, their shirts were pale lavender.

Connor came to a stop beside me. "Do you see Eva anywhere?" I asked.

"Over there," he said.

Eva was one of the girls lying on the ground, her brown curls limp with sweat.

"Eva, what's wrong?" I asked.

She sat up. "Jessica, what are you doing here?" She wore black kneepads and short shorts and clutched a large squirt gun.

I didn't remind her about my non-date with Dominic. "You scared me," I scolded. "I thought something had happened to you."

Shannon walked up and squirted her in the face. "Eva, you're dead. Lie back down."

Obviously, it wasn't sweat in Eva's hair. It was water.

"I'm taking a break," Eva said. She handed Shannon the squirt gun. "I'll be back in ten."

We walked by a couple of the booths on the fairway and Connor bought us snow cones.

"What were all the ambulances for?" I asked.

"A couple of girls fainted. They've been dieting to fit into their homecoming dresses, so the combination of no food and the heat got to them," Eva said. "But Edgar thought we should still go through with the demonstration."

"That seems a little selfish," I said.

"No, just the opposite," Eva insisted. "He's determined to make his mom's store a success. What's more selfless than that?"

It occurred to me that if the store was a success, Edgar could continue to ride in limos and wear expensive clothes.

"There he is," Eva squealed. Edgar, all in white again, was just ahead and she ran to catch up with him. "See you guys later. Have fun!"

The back of her T read SHOOT FOR LOVE, with The Look of Love logo below it, in big purple letters. That was lame. Edgar was turning her into a walking, talking billboard.

She caught up to Edgar and they walked away together hand in hand.

I frowned.

"He's a creep, isn't he?" Connor said. "I hope she doesn't get mixed up with him."

"I think she already is," I said. "She's almost hypnotized when she's around him. It's like no one else even exists."

"Maybe it's love," Connor said softly.

"Maybe," I said. Or maybe it was something else entirely. But what?

We lost sight of them and I was finally able to turn my attention to enjoying the day.

"What do you want to do first?" I asked. There were several stages, many food stands, and lots of games, but I assumed Connor would want to see the headliner band.

"I want to check out Drew Barrymore's Boyfriends," he said. That was a hip local band.

He noticed my surprised expression and said, "Unless there's anything you'd rather do first?"

I put a hand to my forehead. "Uh . . . just gotta send a quick text." I sent Flo a message that it was a false alarm. My tattoo seemed to agree with my assessment and stopped tingling.

Flo texted me back. *Vinnie and I are here, anyway, checking out the competition.*

I put my phone away and then floundered for something to talk about with Connor. "How are your lessons going?" I asked.

"Ms. Minerva says I'm ready for an advanced class. And the jazz band is competing at state soon."

"Congratulations," I said, genuinely impressed.

"You're pretty handy with a guitar yourself," he said. "Have you ever thought about joining a band?"

"I don't like performing in front of people," I confessed. "Besides, it's something that's just for me."

He put an arm around my shoulder. "I get that."

I put a little distance between us. "Let's get something to drink," I said. "My treat." Connor was acting like this was a date, but I'd been stood up by one guy today and wasn't in the mood.

By nightfall, Connor had won a stuffed bear, which he'd promptly given to me. Then we checked out three of the bands. Two of the three weren't as good as Side Effects May Vary, but the other one was amazing.

"Wow," I said when the song ended.

He smiled at me. "I agree completely."

We were walking down the midway when Connor suddenly stopped short. "The picnic!" he said. "I forgot to feed you. You must be starving."

"Not exactly," I said. "Remember? We had snow cones and then we split that turkey leg."

"That was hours ago," he said. "I'll go back to the car to get the cooler. Wait here."

I enjoyed the music while I waited for him to return. That is, until I spotted Selena and Dominic, walking hand in hand. He had her hand in a death grip. Despite the rage that swept through me, I had to admit they looked good together. Dominic had that slightly dazed look a guy sometimes got when he was with a girl he liked.

I was still staring at them when Edgar sidled up next to me.

"Jessica, I like the way you look," he said.

I raised an eyebrow. "So?"

"Ah, of course," he said. "You're beautiful, and therefore you're used to compliments."

"What did you want, Edgar?" I said. He was ruining a perfectly lovely evening with his mere presence.

He handed me a bottle of the "exclusive" perfume everyone had been raving about. I recognized the unusual container.

I handed it back to him. "I'm not interested. In the perfume or you."

He smirked at me, apparently unfazed by my cold shoulder. "I can make you change your mind."

"I doubt it very much," I said.

"So do I," Connor said.

Edgar moved away. "My apologies. Enjoy the rest of the concert."

After he left, Connor asked, "What did he want?"

"I have no idea," I replied. What I really wanted to know was why my tattoo had been throbbing the whole time I talked to Edgar. I passed it off as a combination of my overactive imagination and my dislike of Edgar. After all, how evil could a freshman boy be?

We found a spot not far from the main stage and spread out a blanket Connor had brought, along with a couple of low chairs. He unpacked a delicious meal of veggie sandwiches, potato salad, and sodas, and we ate until we were stuffed. Then we sat back to enjoy more performances.

"This band is good," he said. "Good food, good company. This is the best day I've had since — in a long time." He smiled at me.

We pulled up to my house about five minutes before my curfew. Noel and Harmony waited in the car while Connor walked me to the door.

"Thanks for hanging out with me today," I said.

"I had a great time," Connor said. He grinned. "I don't suppose you'd want to do it again?"

"Connor, there's something I need to tell you."

His grin faded. "That's never good."

"I don't think we should go out anymore." There wasn't any easy way to say it, so I just said it.

"You didn't have fun?"

I put a hand on his arm. "I had a great time, but . . ."

"But you have a thing for Dominic Gray," he said bitterly. "Just like every other girl in Nightshade."

"I was supposed to go out with him today," I confessed. "But he stood me up. And that's when I realized how horrible it was to mess with someone's feelings. I don't want to do that to you."

He didn't say anything for a long time. Finally, he cleared his throat. "I understand, but if you change your mind . . ."

"I won't," I said, but softly.

Mom's face appeared at the front window. I reached over and gave him a peck on the cheek. "I had a wonderful time. Gotta go."

Even though the thing with Connor had ended before it had even really begun, I couldn't wait to tell Eva all about it.

CHAPTER **ELEVEN**

It was between classes on Monday when Dominic decided to try to talk to me.

"Hi, Jessica," he said.

I kept walking, but his longer legs meant he could keep pace with me in the hallway at school.

"Leave me alone," I said.

"What's wrong with you?" he demanded. "I can't believe you're mad at me because I was sick."

"Sick? You are sick. A pathological liar, in fact."

"I had the flu," he said. "I couldn't even get out of bed. The whole weekend was a blur." He raised his voice, which attracted the attention of half of Nightshade High.

"You looked pretty healthy when I saw you hand in hand with Selena," I said.

I marched away, ignoring the stares.

Raven came up to me before class. "What was that all about with my brother?" she asked.

"I don't want to talk about it," I said. I couldn't tell her the truth. That her brother, the great Dominic Gray, was nothing but a liar.

I was home baby-sitting Grace and Katie after school when the doorbell rang. I peered through the peephole and saw Dominic standing on our front porch.

"Oh, now you show up?" I said to him through the door. "Go away."

"Jessica, open up," he pleaded. "I want to talk to you for a minute. To explain."

I opened the door but didn't invite him inside. "You have two minutes."

"I don't remember," he said.

I raised a skeptical eyebrow. "You don't remember what? Asking me out?"

"I remember that," he said. "But this weekend was all a blur. I've been feverish, achy. I thought you saw Selena at the festival with someone who just looked like me. Until . . ."

"Go on," I said.

"Until my own sister told me she saw me there. With Selena. I'm so sorry."

"Do you like her?"

He stared at his feet. Was he embarrassed or lying?

"I don't know." He finally met my eyes. "When I'm not with her, I feel like she's just another girl. Not special. Not you."

Although his last words gave me a thrill, I knew it wasn't enough. "But when you are with her?"

"When I'm with Selena, I can't think of anything or anyone else. It's like magic."

Magic? Something about that word sent up a warning flare in my brain, but I ignored it. Dominic looked so miserable.

I sighed. "Do you want to come in and hang out for a while?" I couldn't believe I was making a move on the guy right after I finally convinced him that I didn't have designs on his hot rock-star body.

He grinned. "Sure."

"My little sisters are home," I warned. "And it'll probably be boring."

"Hey, don't oversell it," he said.

We both laughed.

We found Gracie and Katie in the family room. Gracie didn't even look up from the book she was reading.

"Jessica," Katie said, and launched herself at me. "I'm hungry. Will you play Monopoly with me? Who is that?" The questions came fast and furiously.

"Katie, this is Dominic."

"Is he your boyfriend?" Katie was my favorite little sister or I would have killed her. Instead, I blushed.

"No," I said, so forcefully that Dominic faked a stab to the heart.

"Ha-ha," I said to him, and then turned to Katie. "C'mon, we'll make a snack."

"Monopoly first," she demanded.

"No, snack first," I said firmly.

She skipped ahead of us and climbed onto the barstool in front of the counter that separated the family room from the kitchen.

"Gracie, snack time," I said.

She finally looked up from her book. "Oh, hi, Jessica," she said. "When did you get home?"

I laughed. "It's nice to see you, too, Gracie. Now kitchen. You can read more after your snack. Or maybe you want to play Monopoly with us?"

"No, thank you," she said. Her gaze sharpened. "Who is that?"

I repeated the introduction and she handed me her book before heading for the kitchen.

"I hope you like Monopoly," I said.

"Love it," Dominic said.

"I want banana buddies," Katie demanded. She already had the peanut butter and bread out on the countertop.

"What's that?" Dominic asked.

"Peanut butter on toast with a banana mouth and raisin eyes," I told him.

"My dad used to make us those," he said.

"I can make something else," I said, remembering what Flo had told me about his dad's death.

"No, we can't deprive Katie of her favorite snack. Besides, I like being reminded of him," he said. "I'll make the toast."

Once the toast was made, Katie and Dominic amused each other by decorating the peanut butter with silly faces.

We ate our snack at the kitchen counter. My knee bumped Dominic's under the counter and I jumped.

"Where is everyone else?" I asked Katie. The house was unusually quiet. Not that I was complaining. I could only imagine the grilling I'd get if Sarah and Sydney were home.

"I dunno," she said.

"Katie," I said in a warning voice.

She sighed. "Sarah and Sydney *said* they were at the library studying, but they're probably just giggling about boys. Fiona's at karate and Kellie's at dance class."

Katie went to set up the game and Gracie returned to her book.

"All those girls she mentioned are your sisters?" Dominic asked.

"Every single one," I said. "Are you scared?"

Dominic reached over and slowly rubbed the corner of my mouth with his thumb.

I looked up and met his eyes and a deliciously warm feeling spread through my body. He leaned in and I thought he was going to kiss me.

"You had peanut butter on the corner of your mouth," he said, pulling away.

"Oh," I said. What was I thinking? He could have any girl he wanted. He wasn't interested in me.

Katie's voice shattered the moment. "Jessica, hurry up!" she shouted from the other room.

I gave him a little smile. "This is your chance to make your escape."

"No way," he said. "I love Monopoly."

"Then we'd better get in there," I said. "Katie takes Monopoly very seriously."

"I like you better than that other boy," Katie said to Dominic as she rolled the dice.

He gave me a mischievious glance. "What other boy, Katie?"

"Evan," she said placidly. "He never played Monopoly with me."

"A grave strategic error," Dominic commented.

She nodded. "Exactly."

Dominic didn't seem the least bit intimidated by the thought of competition. If anything, he was amused by it. It felt like he wasn't taking me seriously.

"Are we going to play or what?" I asked.

"It's your turn," Katie pointed out.

"Sorry," I said sheepishly, and then rolled the dice.

I watched him laughing and joking with my sister. Was this the real Dominic? I had thought I was a pretty good judge of character, but it was almost as if there were two of him, Selena's Dominic — the guy who hung on her every word and ignored everyone else around him — and this guy.

CHAPTER TWELVE

I was walking through the halls of Night-shade High when I saw a group of girls surrounding Selena. She handed Shannon something and Shannon let out a squeal.

"Jessica, Jessica, come here," Selena said.

I was kind of stuck. If I didn't do as she asked, I'd look stuck up, but I had a feeling there were strings attached to that particular gift.

"Hi, Selena, what's going on?"

"Tickets to my aunt's new cooking show, *Cooking with the Countess*." She handed me four tickets. "Third-row seats."

"Thanks," I said.

"You'll be there, won't you?" she said.

I glanced at the information on the ticket. It was for Friday night at midnight. "I don't know," I said. "My parents usually don't let me stay out that late."

"Everyone is going to be there," Shannon piped in. "Selena gave tickets to practically everyone in school."

I squared my shoulders. "I'll be there." I'd convince my parents somehow.

I asked Eva to go with me, but she was already going with Edgar and the rest of his perfume groupies. Raven said she'd join me and that we could get a ride there from her brother.

Dominic and Raven picked me up at eleven and came in to say hello to my parents.

"What time will the taping be over?" Dad asked.

"I'm not sure," I replied. "I think it'll be a couple of hours."

"Drive safely," Mom said. "And call us if there's a problem."

We got to the studio early, but a bunch of people we knew were already there.

Eva and Edgar arrived not long after us. Their seats were in the front row, with all his Look of Love groupies, who I'd started to think of as the Lovelies. I wasn't surprised to see they were all wearing purple T-shirts with the store logo, but Edgar had taken it a step further and wore purple jeans.

"I just don't get it," I said.

"You mean, why all those girls hang around him?" Dominic asked.

"That, too," I said. "But mostly I don't get why Eva seems so infatuated."

He shrugged. "The ways of love are strange."

Selena turned around and waved to us, then looked miffed to see Dominic sitting next to me.

When the curtain opened, it revealed an immaculate kitchen stage.

A moment later, music swelled and Circe made a grand entrance. She wore a long black evening gown and matching gloves. Her silver hair was teased into an up do, which was topped by a glittery tiara.

"What's with the ball gown?" Raven whispered. "Not very practical for cooking."

"And satin isn't at all flammable," I whispered back.

An assistant gave Circe a low bow and then wrapped a white apron, trimmed with black bows, around the chef.

She raised one satin glove in the air. "Shall we begin?"

"Begin what?" a voice called out. It was Selena. Clearly a plant.

My suspicion was confirmed when Circe turned a beaming smile upon the audience and said, "Why, making magic, of course."

The crowd roared with approval.

Circe beamed.

I almost forgot about the cameras until the monitors showed a shot of Edgar and Eva kissing.

"Gross," I muttered.

"You have something against kissing?" Raven asked.

"No, something against Edgar," I admitted.

I stopped talking when I felt Circe's strange emerald eyes on me.

"I am making an appetizer, a wonderful soup to start, a main course, and a special dessert," she announced. "This is a dessert created for my husband, the Count, for our three-month anniversary."

She had a commanding presence and clearly knew her way around the kitchen, but I felt uneasy. The sound of shattering glass came from backstage somewhere.

Some guy with a clipboard signaled to the assistant and the taping stopped abruptly.

The two conferred briefly and then went to investigate. A few minutes later, the assistant was back. Obviously, she'd gotten the short end of the stick, because she dragged her feet all the way to Circe.

Whatever she said, Circe looked like she was going to explode. Selena hurried up to her aunt and put a hand on her arm, and then Circe turned with a broad smile to the watching audience. "There will be a slight delay," she said through gritted teeth. "Please enjoy a delicious complimentary appetizer while we address this minor glitch."

Despite her reassurances, the appetizer was not delicious and the delay was not slight. We waited for over an hour. The assistant scurried around and served the audience, but the demand exceeded her speediness. Selena finally took pity on her and started handing out appetizers, too. She came over to offer us some from a tray.

"These are from my aunt's secret recipe," she said.

"Thank you," I said politely as I took one. There were little *oohs* and *ahhs* of delight from the crowd, but when I bit into mine, I had to restrain myself from spitting it out.

"It tastes horrible," I whispered to Raven.

"It can't be that bad," she replied. She took a big bite and then spit it out in the little cocktail napkin Selena had given her. "It's worse."

"Shhh! She'll hear you," I cautioned.

Everyone else was eating the snack with every appearance of enjoyment.

Dominic hadn't tried his yet. He held it up and sniffed it delicately, then put it down. "I'm not sure I want to try it after the reaction you two had."

Selena was heading back our way. "Do you want another one?" she said. "My aunt wants to make sure everyone gets at least one."

"What's in it?" Dominic asked.

"I can't tell you the ingredients. It's from her new cookbook. Top secret." She looked over her shoulder nervously.

He handed the appetizer back to her. "Sorry, I have allergies. Can't be too careful."

"I guess it will be okay to tell you some of the ingredients," Selena said. "Black truffles, porcini, and goat cheese crostini."

"Aren't truffles mushrooms?" Dominic asked. "That's what I'm allergic to."

"You wouldn't want him to get sick or anything," I said.

"Oh, you're right. Aunt Circe wouldn't want anyone to get sick on her show," Selena said. "Thanks, Jessica."

After she moved on to serve the rest of the audience, I turned to Dominic. "I didn't know you were allergic to mushrooms," I said.

"You caught me," he said.

"You're a good liar," I said. I wasn't sure that was a trait to look for in a potential boyfriend.

"I'm not a good liar," Dominic said. "Ask Raven."

She nodded. "He usually turns red and gets all twitchy. Like that," she said, pointing at Dominic's tomato-red face.

"So why did you lie?" I asked.

"I didn't want to hurt her feelings," he said.

I tried not to let it show, but I was annoyed. I should be happy that he was sensitive enough to think of Selena's feelings, but I wanted him to care about me, not her.

I turned my attention back to the stage. Circe was finally getting ready to prepare the soup. "I'm making a delicious potato leek soup today," she announced.

"Brooke, where is my food processor? Brooke, you stupid girl," she said, loud enough for the audience to hear.

When she saw that the audience was staring at her with stunned disbelief, she changed her tone. "Brooke, please bring me the food processor, will you?"

The harried assistant ran onstage with a large food processor. "The leeks, dear girl," Circe said, gritting her teeth.

Circe watched Brooke as she chopped the leeks and potatoes. Then Circe put the items in the food processor, poured a healthy portion of cream into the mix, and hit the button.

The utensil whirled and whirled and a strange green fog formed. The noise grew so loud that I clapped my hands over my ears, and then the top of the lid exploded and a food tornado formed over the blender.

"Is this part of the show?" Raven whispered.

"I don't think so," I said.

The funnel cloud grew darker and gained speed. It grew larger and larger until it loomed over the transfixed audience.

"I think we should get out of here," Dominic said. He took my hand and pulled me up. "When that thing blows, it's going to be a mess."

We inched our way to the aisle, and the funnel cloud stopped spinning. Potatoes, leeks, and cream rained down upon everyone in the room. Pellets of food hit with the force of hail.

There were chunks of potato and dairy product in my hair.

"I need a shower," I said.

"I need about twelve showers," Raven replied.

"This is an outrage!" someone shouted. "What kind of cooking show is this?"

Circe looked like she was ready to explode, just like the potato leek soup.

"Brooke," Circe's voice rang out loud and clear. "You fool, what are you waiting for? Clean this mess up now!"

Staff members handed out towels and apologies, but it wasn't enough to get anyone to stay. As the audience filtered out, an older gentleman yelled, "You'll be hearing from my attorney."

Raven bent over and shook the gunk out of her hair. "Well, that was a disaster," she said cheerfully.

It was, but I wondered why it had happened. Potato funnel clouds didn't happen every day, which meant magic had been used. The only two witches I knew were Selena and Circe, and I couldn't think of any reason they'd want to ruin the performance.

Someone was sabotaging Circe's new cooking show, but why?

After we left, Raven said, "I just got a text from Aunt Katrina. She's at Slim's. She wants to stop for ice cream."

Dominic looked to me. "Do you want to come along, Jess?"

I nodded. "Ice cream sounds good."

"Then ice cream it is," Dominic said.

Nurse Phillips wasn't nearly as intimidating when she was out of the naughty nurse outfit that she wore onstage, along with a variety of outrageous wigs and dramatic makeup.

She sat across from me in a vintage Cabbage Patch T-shirt and jeans. I could see a resemblance to Dominic. They had the same blond hair and up tilted eyes.

"You two look alike," I commented.

"I'm assuming you aren't talking about me," Raven said. Raven was small, with dark hair.

"You all have the same-shaped eyes," I said. "But Nurse Phillips and Dom really look alike. Same hair, same high cheekbones, same—"

Dominic cut me off. "Raven looks like my dad." He abruptly got up from the table and went to the jukebox. The set of his shoulders told me he wanted to be left alone.

I stared after him, astonished. "What did I say?"

"Dominic resembles his mother," Nurse Phillips said gently. "My sister."

I was still lost, but he came back before I had the chance to ask any more questions. "Sorry," he said. "Just needed a minute."

We finished our ice cream and then called it a night. Raven got a ride with her aunt, and Dominic drove me home. He didn't say anything on the way back to my house.

I cleared my throat. "How do you like living in Nightshade so far?" I asked politely. To be honest, I wasn't sure how to talk to him.

"It's definitely growing on me," he said. "At first I didn't want to leave my friends, but it wasn't like I had any choice."

"It must be tough to lose both of your parents," I said. "How long ago did your mom die?"

"My mom has been gone for three years," he said. "Look, it's not something I like to talk about. Can we change the subject?"

"Of course," I said. I felt like an idiot for bringing it up. I get five seconds alone with him, and instead of flirting, I bring up the most depressing topic possible.

Neither of us said another word until we reached my house. "Thanks for the ride," I said, my hand already on the door. He probably couldn't wait to get away from me. "I'm sorry I asked so many dumb questions."

He reached for my hand. "Jessica, wait a minute."

"I've got to go," I replied. "It's past my curfew."

"Look, I'm sorry if I was a jerk, but the subject of my mom is off-limits," he said. "It's too painful to talk about, okay?"

"Okay," I said. "I understand, but I've got to go."

It was true. I could see my dad's silhouette in the window.

But after I went inside, I couldn't help but wonder if I was up to going out with a boy who had so many secrets.

CHAPTER THIRTEEN

Side Effects May Vary had another gig at the Black Opal and Raven had asked me to go with her. The place was packed. There were a lot of girls in the audience. A lot of *cute* girls.

Nurse Phillips wore a bright pink wig, six-inch platform shoes, and a white plastic dress.

"Your aunt is amazing," I told Raven as I watched Nurse Phillips strum her guitar.

Dominic's outfit was a little more low-key than his aunt's. Tight black jeans and an orange T-shirt that made his eyes look even bluer. When he came onstage, the squeals from the girls were nearly deafening. He saw us in the front row and gave a little wave before he started the first song.

A strange look crossed his face and then he went glassy-eyed.

"He's doing it again," Raven said under her breath.

Dominic usually focused on the audience, but his gaze

was centered somewhere above their heads, at a distant point on some imaginary horizon. He looked seriously zoned out. I swear I saw his eyes go back in his head, just for a second.

And then he started to sing. I didn't recognize the song, but Raven identified it for me. "Oh, no. He's singing 'Love Potion Number Nine.'"

"What do you think it means?" I asked.

"Maybe Dominic will talk to you about it. It seems like you two have become close lately."

"Does that bother you?" I wanted to know because Raven was supposed to have my back in the event of a big fight and I didn't want her mad at me.

"Of course not," she said. "I want him to be happy. It's just that . . ." She didn't finish her sentence. "He's been acting weird lately."

Dominic had been acting weird. I knew girls blamed other girls all the time, but something wasn't right with him. He claimed to not remember going out with Selena in the first place. Dominic was a star in Nightshade. He could have any girl he wanted. Sometimes it was clear to me that he'd chosen Selena, but other times, I felt that he really might like me. Either I was completely wrong about him and he was playing us, or there was something fishy going on.

I turned my attention back to the stage. The band

was struggling to keep up with him. The crowd didn't seem to notice, but I'd overheard their band practice enough to know that the song wasn't on the set list. When the song ended, the crowd let out a roar of approval.

Dominic could do no wrong with his fans, but his band mates were another matter. As soon as the song ended, Nurse Phillips announced a short break. Before she'd even finished, Vinnie had stalked offstage.

Katrina went up to Dominic and put a comforting arm on his shoulder, but he shrugged it off and made his own stormy exit.

"I'll be right back," I told Raven. "I'm going to go talk to him."

I found him outside, sitting on a low wall behind the back door.

"I don't know why it happens!" he burst out when he saw me. "So don't bug me about it."

"I wasn't going to bug you," I said. "I was going to see if I could help, but you obviously don't want my help." I turned around and started to march off.

"Wait, Jessica," he said, but I kept moving. "Please?" he added.

I stopped and faced him. "I don't need a jerk in my life," I said. "I thought you were different."

"I apologize," he said. "I'm upset and I took it out on you."

"Apology accepted," I replied. "But this moody rockstar stuff that may work with other girls doesn't work with me. I'm trying to be your friend."

"I know," he said, and took my hand.

I tried to ignore the way my heartbeat accelerated. "So you don't have any idea why it happens?" I asked.

"None," he said. "It's driving the other band members crazy, and I don't blame them."

"Do the songs mean something to you?" I asked.

He shrugged. "I don't think so. It's only happened a few times, but that's too often as far as Jeff's concerned. He didn't want me in the band even before this started to happen."

"Why not?" I asked.

"I'm just a kid, at least according to him," Dominic replied. "Aunt Katrina convinced him to give me a chance, and now this."

"Did it ever happen before you moved to Nightshade?"

He shook his head. "The first time it happened was a few weeks ago. Out of nowhere, I started to sing 'Ant Music.'"

"'Ant Music'? By Adam and the Ants?" I asked.

He raised his eyebrows. "You know that song?"

"My brother, Sean, dressed like Adam Ant for an 'eighties night dance once," I explained.

"Well, we don't do covers of Adam and the Ants," he said flatly. "And the night we met — let's just say 'Crazy for You' isn't in the band's repertoire."

"Is that why you were such a . . ." My voice trailed off. No sense in kicking him when he was down.

"Jerk?" He finished my sentence. "Yep. I was freaked out and I took it out on you. Sorry."

"Nightshade does bring out the strange in people," I said. "Look, I think you should talk to the band and let them know you're not trying to — "

"Be an egomaniacal pain in the butt?" he finished for me. "I can do that."

"And that we're trying to figure it out," I said. "Maybe they could learn a few more songs."

He nodded. "It's better than anything I've come up with on my own."

We walked back to the club. There wasn't much else I could say to him. The band finished their performance without any more random songs, but I could tell Jeff Cool wasn't cool about it.

◆ ◆ ◆

At lunch the next day, I grabbed my tray and looked for

someone to sit with. Eva was already at a table with Shannon and the rest of Edgar's Lovelies.

To their left, Dominic sat by himself. He was wearing a Nightshade High hooded sweatshirt, with the hood up. He was obviously avoiding his fans. His whole body screamed, "Leave me alone."

I spotted Raven and Andy and went to sit with them instead.

"Avoiding my brother?" Raven asked.

I shrugged. "He seems to want to be alone."

"You should go talk to him," Raven said softly.

I glanced back at him. "I'll be right back," I said.

I went to Dominic's table and sat next to him. "Is this seat taken?"

"I thought you might be avoiding me," he said.

"Why would I avoid you?"

"Because I'm a freak," he said.

"You're not a freak," I replied. "You're just . . . different."

"Yeah, and we both know how well different goes over in high school."

"Nightshade High isn't like most high schools," I told him.

"What do you mean?"

I hesitated. I didn't want to sound like a complete

loon, but maybe it could help him. "The city of Night-shade is home to several paranormals," I finally said.

"You mean witches and vampires and stuff?" he asked. "I know."

"You know?" I repeated.

"Aunt Katrina told us all about it before we came to live with her," he said. "She wanted us to be prepared."

"I'm not sure there is a way to prepare for living in Nightshade," I told him. "But I'm glad you're here."

"I'm glad I'm here, too," he said. "Especially now that I've met you."

We smiled at each other, for once in perfect harmony.

CHAPTER FOURTEEN

I'd joined the high school show choir at Eva's behest, the only elective that would fit with soccer. And even though I was only a freshman, Mom was already encouraging me to join clubs in order to look good on my college applications.

We didn't have a very good choir. It wasn't that we couldn't carry a tune or anything, but we just hadn't had enough practice. Or even enough members. Our choral director, Ms. Clare, had a reputation for being moody, and she expected perfection from every single member. Not that she got it, from me, at least.

Ms. Clare had dark brown hair that she parted in the middle and then tortured in to a high bun at the back of her neck. She always wore smocklike tops with a pattern of music notes. Or when she got dressed up, a severe black suit and a SING OUT LOUD brooch pinned to the collar.

It was only our third practice and things seemed to be progressing nicely between Eva and Evan. They'd walked to the music room together every time so far. Still, she kept staring at Edgar.

"Who would like to try out for a solo?" Ms. Clare asked. Harmony Clare was the only one to raise her hand. Ms. Clare frowned, but nodded. "Take your place at the microphone, Harmony. And this time, try to stay in tune."

We didn't have any stand-out soloists, but Harmony, who was Ms. Clare's daughter, had already tried out several times. Unfortunately, her name didn't match her singing skills.

I crossed my fingers that her singing had improved, but when she tried and failed to hit the high notes, it was clear she hadn't.

Wolfgang Paxton let out a howl of laughter, but he stopped abruptly when Ms. Clare looked his way.

I tried to hide my winces, but Wolfie didn't even bother hiding his contempt. Why was he in show choir, anyway?

I figured it out when I spotted his girlfriend, Claudia Dracul, standing next to him.

"Why don't we ask the Little Mermaid to try out for a solo?" a guy's voice called out. I was the only redhead in choir, so I knew he was talking about me. I turned to see who was speaking. It was Tim, my stocky stalker from the first day.

He smirked at me and I smirked back. "Actually, Tim, Ariel gives up her voice for love," Eva said. "So your logic, as usual, is faulty."

How did she know him? I shot her a puzzled glance and she mouthed, "HACC," back at me. I couldn't figure out what she meant until I remembered what HACC stood for, Horror and Cinema Club. I was very glad that Eva hadn't convinced me to sign up for that club, too. Seeing Tim once a week was more than enough for me.

Ms. Clare obviously planned to remedy the lack of talent in our show choir because when Dominic and Raven walked into the choir room, she was all smiles.

"Sorry we're late," Dominic said.

Eva nudged me in the ribs. "Wonder why he's suddenly so interested in show choir?" she said in a whisper.

"Oh, I don't know," I said. "Maybe because he's a singer."

"Class, class, settle down," Ms. Clare said, even though no one was talking. "I am so pleased to announce that Dominic and Raven Gray will be joining the chorus. Dominic will be trying out for a solo."

"Do you know the words to 'I'm an Ordinary Man'?" she asked him.

He nodded and she sat at the piano and began to play the song from *My Fair Lady*, which we'd been practicing since school had begun.

Dominic started to sing the words, but then his face changed. His jaw went slack and I knew right away that he was not going to be singing the song she had requested.

Instead, the words to "Killer Queen" came out of his mouth. The other kids started laughing, probably thinking that he was clowning around for their amusement, but I knew the truth. His eyes rolled back.

Ms. Clare stopped playing and sat there staring at him. She frowned deeply and a *You're going to the principal's office* expression appeared on her face. She was an old-school choir director and didn't like any music that was created after 1970.

"Do something," Raven hissed.

I hated calling attention to myself, but I couldn't let Dominic crash and burn. "Follow my lead," I said. I went to the microphone and started to sing along with him. After an agonizingly long verse, Raven joined in and the three of us sang the rest of the song a cappella.

When we finished, there was a long silence, and then the room burst into applause.

"What a wonderful . . . performance," Ms. Clare said lamely.

"We thought maybe we could do something different this year," I said.

"I'll take it under consideration," she said. But I knew

she wouldn't. We'd be singing the same stale stuff all year, but I didn't care, as long as Dominic was okay.

Ms. Clare's eyes began to gleam. "Maybe we will find a song suitable for a duet."

"I want to try out for the duet," Janie Clark said.

"Me, too," another voice said.

"Who else would like to try out for the duet?" Ms. Clare asked.

Several hands were raised. All of them belonged to girls.

"Let's take a five-minute break," Ms. Clare said. "And then we'll get back to practice."

Raven, Dominic, and I took advantage of the break for an emergency huddle.

Dominic gave my hand a grateful squeeze. "Thanks," he said in a low voice. "You saved me back there."

"What are we going to do if it happens again?" Raven asked in a whisper.

"It won't," I said with more confidence than I felt.

"Maybe I should just quit," Dominic said.

Ms. Clare, who had been hovering nearby, overheard him. "No, no," she said. "I am honored to have such talent in my little choir room, no matter what songs you sing."

I had an idea and I hoped it would work, at least enough to get her off his back. "Dom is a true artist," I said theatrically. I sounded pompous even to my own ears. "He isn't able to conform to a strict song list. He needs freedom to sing the songs his muse demands."

"And he shall have it!" Ms. Clare said. Then in a low voice, she added, "Please don't quit the choir. We need your voice."

Dominic looked like he was going to burst into laughter at my over-the-top speech, but managed to spit out, "I'll stay."

After choir practice, he was swept away by a group of his fans, and Eva and Evan came over to join me.

"Thanks for sticking up for me with Tim," I said to her. "Do you know how many times I've heard that Little Mermaid reference?"

"Tim's a jerk," Eva said promptly. "He doesn't even like Vincent Price movies — can you believe it?"

"You like Vincent Price?" Evan said. "Me, too!"

They started talking the merits of *The House of Usher* versus *The Pit and the Pendulum* and I zoned out for a few minutes.

"I've got to go or I'll be late for practice," Evan said. "But I'll call you later."

After he left, I said, "That sounds promising."

"He's great," Eva said. "But Edgar is cuter." I groaned inwardly at that, but didn't say anything. We talked — or,

I should say, *she* talked—about Edgar's many wonderful qualities until we parted ways at the bus stop. It was nice to see Eva so happy, even though I thought Edgar was a creep.

It was standing room only at the next chorus practice. I spotted Bethany and Tiffany and a bunch of other junior girls. There were even a few senior girls there, most of whom couldn't even carry a tune. Dominic and I walked in together, but he was immediately surrounded, while I was shoved aside.

There were definitely negatives to crushing on a rock star.

Raven came to join me in the corner. "They're like a pack of wild beasts fighting over a juicy T-bone."

"Has it always been like this?" I asked. "The fans, I mean."

"Not at all," she said. "Before he was in the band, he was just kind of quiet. You're the first girl he's ever been interested in. I was surprised about that."

Before I had a chance to ask her what she meant by that, Ms. Clare came in and started the class.

There was a waiting list for trying out for the duets. Bethany and Tiffany nearly came to blows when they were passing around the sign-up sheet. But for the rest of chorus practice, I thought about what Raven had said, wondering what she had meant. Why was it surprising that Dominic would be interested in me?

Then I spotted him leaving the music room with Selena, and realized it wasn't me he was interested in.

CHAPTER FIFTEEN

Friday night, Dominic called me and asked me to meet him at a sound check at the Black Opal.

"I don't think so, Dominic," I told him. "I'm really not into game playing."

"I'm *not* playing games," he said. "I need to talk to you about what's happening to me. There's something wrong, Jessica, I just know it."

"I guess. I already told Flo I'd meet her there later, anyway."

When I arrived, the rest of the band wasn't there yet. There was one lonely server filling the napkin holders.

Dominic and I sat at one of the tables and waited for the others to show up.

"Do you guys want something to drink?" the server asked. She smiled at Dominic when she said it.

"A couple of Cokes would be great," he replied.

When she brought back our drinks, I pointed to the Warhol-style painting I'd noticed before. "Who is that?"

She set our frosted glasses on the table. "That's the owner," she said. "You've never seen her in here? Or the old place?"

"No, I've never seen her," I replied, as the server walked away.

"You wanted to talk to me about something?" I prompted Dominic.

"I want you to observe me the next time I'm hanging out with Selena."

"What? No way."

"I know it's asking a lot, but I need your help."

"Dominic, I don't think it's a good idea," I protested. "Can't Raven do it?"

"She's mad at me right now."

"Raven? I didn't think she ever got mad," I said.

"She's mad all right," he told me.

"About what?"

"She thinks I'm making excuses about Selena to you," he said. "But I'm not. Something's not right. I feel woozy when I'm with her. And not in a good way."

"'Woozy'?"

"Lightheaded, kind of sick to my stomach," he replied.

Could Selena be the one responsible for his symptoms? Or was Dominic uncomfortable with his own feelings?

The door opened and a short woman with dark hair

and purple highlights walked through it. She carried a guitar case.

She marched right over to our table. "You the lead singer of Side Effects May Vary?" she asked Dominic.

"Yes, m'am, I am," he said.

"Then why aren't you singing?" she said. "Isn't there a sound check scheduled for today?"

"Yes, there is," Dominic said. "But the rest of the band is running late."

She seemed to realize she'd been a little abrupt. "I'm Teddie Myles," she said. "I own this place."

I recognized her as the woman in the portrait I had asked about earlier.

"I'll play my guitar while you sing." She opened the case and as she got out her guitar, I noticed her tattoo. It was unusual, a peace sign morphing into a mushroom cloud. She caught me staring.

"I got this in 1964," she said. "Protesting nuclear testing."

"I like it," I said.

Her gaze focused on my bicep. "I like yours, too."

I squirmed and grabbed my hoodie, to cover up my arm.

As she headed for the stage, she added, "You're too young for a tattoo."

I had a tattoo, but it wasn't like I'd picked it out or

anything. I was growing fond of my whirlwind, but I wasn't ready to show it to the world.

Dominic finished his soda, then went to the stage. He conferred with Teddie briefly and began singing something I'd never heard before. Teddie sang backup in a raspy, timeworn voice that made me think of long lonely road trips.

But I was riveted by Dominic's performance. He sang this song with his eyes closed, maybe with the hope of preventing any oracular revelations. But the intensity and passion in his voice sent shivers down my spine.

My reverie was interrupted when the rest of the band entered the club — Flo, too, holding hands with her boyfriend. Dominic stopped in the middle of the chorus. "Looks like everyone is here," he said.

Teddie packed up her guitar and headed back to where I sat. "He's got something special, doesn't he?" she commented.

"Yes, he certainly does," I replied.

She handed me a small white card with her name and number printed on it. "I've got to head out," she said. "But, Jessica, if you ever need anything, give me a call."

"Thanks, I will." How did she know my name? I was almost certain I hadn't introduced myself.

After Teddie left, Dominic sat back down while the

rest of the band set up their instruments. "I can't believe it! I just sang with Teddie Myles," he gushed.

"She seems nice," I said cautiously. I was clearly missing something.

"Nice? The legendary Teddie Myles is more than nice," he replied. "She's — she's . . ."

"Legendary?"

"You mean you don't know who Teddie Myles is?" Selena had come into the club without my even noticing. She seemed to be spending a lot of time hanging around.

"And I suppose you do?" I asked.

"As a matter of fact, I do," she said. "Dominic told me all about it the other night."

The other night? I shot him a sharp glance, but he only smiled blandly at her. "Selena was helping me channel my powers," he said. "Remember?"

"Why don't you enlighten me?" I asked. Despite her know-it-all attitude, I noticed she waited for Dominic to fill me in.

"Teddie Myles is a legend," Dominic said. "She was the lead singer in Temptation and then she had this amazing solo career."

"Dominic, when you're done chatting with your groupies, would you care to join us onstage?" Jeff Cool said sarcastically.

Groupies?

"Jessica and Selena aren't groupies, Jeff," Dominic snapped. "I expect you to show my friends respect."

"We'd better let you rehearse," I said.

"Hang on a sec, Jessica," Dominic said. "Selena, thanks for everything."

He'd made it clear — politely, of course — that he wanted Selena to leave, but she didn't budge.

"Dominic, pay attention to me," Selena said. Her voice sounded like a whiny five-year-old's. Then she picked up his hand and repeated her words. But when she said it the second time, she sounded loud and full of power.

Jeff grumbled some more about high-maintenance singers, but Dominic ignored him.

Flo gave me a look.

I didn't want to hang around for rehearsal any longer. I had tried to ignore Jeff's groupie comment, but it stung. Is that how everyone saw me? Just some girl who hung all over Dominic because he was in a band?

To make matters worse, Selena still had Dominic's hand and he was all gooey-eyed over her.

"Don't let Jeff bother you," Flo said. "He's a misogynist."

"I have more important things to worry about," I said with false bravado. But it was true. Things were murky indeed, and I couldn't seem to figure out how to clear them up.

CHAPTER SIXTEEN

I wanted to lounge around on Saturday morning before virago training, but Mom had other plans for me.

"Jessica, the laundry is really piling up," she said.

"I thought Poppy was going to start working here."

"To help me with paperwork and your little sisters," Mom replied. "Not do your chores." She used that *We're done talking about it* tone that all moms seemed to have.

"Isn't it about time that Fiona did her own laundry?" I complained. Sean, Sarah, Sydney, and I all had to do our own laundry, but that still left Fiona, Grace, Kellie, and Katie.

As soon as I'd hit sixth grade, Mom and Dad had given me a guided tour of the laundry room, and the washer and dryer had been my almost constant companions ever since.

Mom actually considered it for a few seconds before

the veto came. "Maybe you can show her the ropes next month," she said.

I knew I'd never get out of the house if I tried to argue, so I made my way to the laundry space and stared at the piles of clothes until I had a bright idea. I sorted everything and put the first load in before I went to find my sister Sarah.

"I'll give you wardrobe privileges for a week if you do the rest of the laundry," I said.

She looked up from her computer and her eyes gleamed with avarice. "Including your new stuff?"

When Mom had finally taken us back-to-school shopping, I had found some killer outfits. I hadn't even worn some of the clothes yet, but I nodded.

"Make it two weeks and it's a deal," she said.

I looked at the clock. There was no way I would get out of the house in time to make it to training unless I agreed. I nodded.

"Is it true that you have a thing for Dominic Gray?"

I frowned. "He's been spending a lot of time with Selena Silvertongue."

"Like that's going to last," she scoffed. "Gabi's sister says that it doesn't seem like he's into her most of the time." Gabi was Sarah's best friend. Gabi's sister was a junior, like Dominic.

Sarah yawned. "Gabi's sister says he only acts inter-ested when Selena hangs all over him."

Maybe Dominic wasn't lying to me about what he said at the Black Opal the day before. It dawned on me that his weird behavior could be more than the typi-cal confusion of a first love. Maybe it wasn't natural at all. Selena was a sorceress. But what did that mean exactly?

"Dominic and I are just friends," I replied. "Although I might see him at training."

"Training?" She pounced on my slip.

I panicked as I tried to think of an answer. "Yeah," I finally choked out. "His sister, Raven, is helping me train."

"For soccer?" She gave me a skeptical look. "Since when do you need extra training sessions?"

The one thing I had in common with my brother was my athletic ability. Dad said I was just born with it, which, if you think about it, was less than flattering. It's not a talent. It's just something I had, like red hair.

"Coach McGill is a lot tougher than all my previous coaches put together." I put a hand on my hip and hoped she'd believe my cover story.

Sarah seemed to lose interest in my love life, thank-fully, but followed me to the laundry room. "That's more than one week's worth of laundry," she accused.

"I know, I know," I said. "I'll make it up to you."

"You'd better," Sarah said menacingly.

I scampered out the door before the last threat was out of her mouth.

I arrived at the Mason house out of breath. There was no sign of any of the other viragos in the backyard, but I could hear voices coming from the living room. The band had hauled in an old couch and chair and scattered a few beanbags on the floor. They were probably all waiting for me in there.

Instead, I found Selena and Dominic sitting on the sofa, holding hands.

"Sorry!" I said, before turning around and rushing out.

Dominic caught up with me before I made it to the front porch. "Jessica, wait," he said. "It's not what it looked like."

"It's none of my business," I replied.

"I'm hoping that it is," he said. He squeezed my hand, but I jerked it away. "Selena was helping me with my . . . gift."

I raised an eyebrow. "Is that what they're calling it these days?"

"You're jealous," he said. He smiled at me, clearly delighted.

"Stop smiling like that," I said.

"Like what?" he said innocently.

I couldn't help it. I started to laugh.

He laughed, too, but sobered quickly.

"What happens when Selena helps you to control your powers?"

"We hold hands," he said. Then he added quickly, "She says it helps to create a connection."

"Then what?" Something was bothering me about the whole thing, but I couldn't pinpoint what bothered me exactly. It wasn't just jealousy.

There was a look of confusion on his face. "Then it gets a bit fuzzy."

I looked into his eyes expectantly, waiting for him to go on.

"I'd like to get to know you better, Jessica," he blurted out.

After Dominic's confession, we were quiet for a minute. I could tell he was waiting for me to say something.

"I'd like to get to know you better, too," I finally said. "But you and Selena . . ."

A cloud crossed over his face. "No buts," he replied. "We want to spend time together. That's all that matters."

Easy for him to say. He didn't have to face Selena's friends and their death stares. Or his more persistent fans.

He grabbed my hand. "Now come back inside. Raven told me to let you know that she and Flo were going to be late. They should be here soon."

We went back inside, but there was no sign of Selena. Had she overheard what Dominic had said?

"Where did Selena go?" Dominic asked. He didn't sound too broken-hearted about her absence, though, and I had to suppress my glee.

There was a guitar in the corner, so I picked it up. I needed to practice or Ms. Minerva was going to drop me as her student.

I strummed a few chords of "Again," by Lenny Kravitz. Dominic sat next to me and watched as I played, but only seconds into the song, his eyes rolled back in his head. He softly sang the lyrics to Bryan Ferry's "Slave to Love."

When the song was over, Dominic returned to normal. "It happened again, didn't it?" he asked.

I nodded.

"What did I sing?"

He winced when I told him. "I have no idea what that means."

I guess he was bummed Selena had left. He was obviously slavishly in love with her. The green-eyed monster had quickly become a regular visitor in my brain.

It was an odd feeling, but I put it out of my mind when Flo and Raven arrived, followed almost immediately by Andy.

What had my fellow viragos been doing without me? I felt a twinge of jealousy, this time the professional kind. They were all carrying take-out containers from Slim's.

"Surprise," Flo said. "Training has been canceled for the day." Her T-shirt read I PUT THE FATAL IN FEMME FATALE.

"Canceled? Why?" I asked.

Flo turned a stern gaze on me and said, "Because I say so."

"Oh, great," I said.

It was hard to tell with Flo, but I think she actually looked pleased with herself, so I didn't have the heart to complain. But I'd just traded a serious favor to get some training in. I'd have to squeeze in a run at night.

"Something smells delicious," Vinnie said as he walked in. He put his arms around Flo's waist.

"I brought lunch for everybody," Flo announced. He buried his face in her neck and then whispered something that made her blush.

She wiggled out of his arms. "Not in front of the children," she said. But they were both grinning.

I looked over at Raven meaningfully. It hadn't escaped our notice that training just happened to be always scheduled the same time as band practice.

"True love," she said. I tried not to look at Dominic when she said it.

We put everything on the kitchen counter.

"Slim sent along a cheesecake, too," Flo said.

"Oh, be sure to thank him for me," I said.

"Cheesecake is my favorite," Dominic said. "So thank him for me, too."

"You can thank him yourself," Flo said. "Because here he comes."

I took her word for it.

Slim and his fiancée, Natalie, came in with even more food.

"This isn't lunch, it's a feast!" Andy said. She peeked into the containers. "Oh, yum. Spinach salad."

It seemed like there was a little bit of everything to eat.

The rest of the band arrived and gladly joined us. It was a little crowded in the kitchen, but Natalie told us there was a large patio table and chairs in the backyard, so we took the food outside.

Jeff Cool reached over and took almost all the crab legs. I gave him a dirty look. I loved crab. Dominic took some of the crab legs off his plate and gave them to me.

"I don't like them that much, anyhow," he said.

"What's the special occasion?" Nurse Phillips asked.

"I was wondering the same thing," Raven said.

"Just experimenting with a new menu," Slim said. "And you all are my guinea pigs."

"The experiment was a success," Raven replied. She leaned back and patted her stomach contentedly.

"Speaking of food," Flo said, "I heard there was another disaster on Circe Silvertongue's cooking show."

"Selena told me everything," Andy said importantly. "The *Cooking with Circe* show was taping last night. Circe was preparing cherries jubilee flambé and the place caught on fire. But there was no way it was an accident."

"Did someone tamper with the cooking tools?" I asked.

"Worse," Andy said. "Selena said someone used magic to wreck the show. There was a food critic there and everything."

"You left out the part where the place nearly burned to the ground," Flo said dryly.

"It wasn't quite that bad," Andy said. "Dominic put out the fire with an ice bucket."

"Dominic was there?" I wished I hadn't said it as soon as the words escaped.

Andy shot me a dirty look. "He *is* Selena's boyfriend."

"That's not what he says," Raven muttered under her

breath. Andy gave her a sharp look, but Raven just smiled at her innocently.

"But who sabotaged the show?" I said. "And why?"

Andy shrugged.

I took a slice of cheesecake and was in heaven after one bite. "This is so good. Thanks, Slim."

"Don't thank me," he replied. "Daisy made it."

"'Daisy'?" I repeated. The girl could do everything *and* she had Ryan Mendez. Life wasn't fair.

"Daisy Giordano," he clarified. "Isn't she your neighbor?"

"Yes," I said. "But I don't see her very often now that she's in college," I added.

"Maybe Daisy can help you with your problem," Slim suggested. "She worked with Circe last summer."

"This is a virago issue," Flo said. "We need to figure it out ourselves. Daisy is busy and she's been through a lot."

And then there was a painful silence as we remembered the explosion, the chief's death, and Daisy's hospitalization.

"I'm going to have to go for a jog later," I said brightly, ignoring the tension in the room.

"Maybe I'll join you," Dominic said.

"I'd like that."

Raven snorted. "Dom, Jessica can run a four-minute mile."

"Your point?" he said, but he gave me a sidelong look.

"You complain if the remote is too far away for you to reach it," she replied. "There's no way you'll be able to keep up with her."

"Speaking of running," Andy said. "Look."

She pointed to the adjoining yard. The sun was so bright that I couldn't see, so I shaded my eyes. Miss McBennett's St. Bernard puppy bounded by with a large meaty bone in his mouth.

Jaci Kelley followed the puppy. "Come here," she growled. There was a little bit of drool hanging from the corner of her mouth. "Give it to me."

While we watched in amazement, Jaci wrestled the bone from the dog and started to gnaw on it. She wore oversized sunglasses with a grubby sundress and mismatched shoes. Not her usual look at all.

"Gross," Jeff said, and then returned to his food like it was an everyday occurrence to see a teenage girl chewing on a dog bone.

"We should stop her," Nurse Phillips said. "She could get sick from eating raw meat."

I was sitting near Flo, so I heard her low-voiced conversation with her brother.

"Werewolf?" Slim asked.

"Did you see the palms of her hands?" Flo asked. "They're bright red."

The palms of her hands? Why was that significant?

"I'm afraid you have another problem on your hands."

"Don't say it," Flo begged.

But he did. "Zombies."

I knew that where there was one zombie, there were many, many more. Nightshade was in trouble and my tattoo hadn't even tingled.

CHAPTER SEVENTEEN

The next day, I looked for her in every class, but Jaci wasn't in school.

I was walking from English to Geometry when I spotted Dominic in the hallway. I started to go over to say hi, but then I noticed that Selena was standing next to him.

They both waved at me. I waved back like I didn't have a care in the world, but inside, I was fuming.

After my last class, I went to find Eva. We still walked home together, even though Edgar seemed to be taking up most of her time these days. Not surprisingly, he was at her locker. As I watched, he leaned in. I thought he was going to kiss her, but instead he seemed to be smelling her. He seemed to be reprimanding her about something, then walked away.

"Do you think something happened to Jaci?" I asked Eva as we walked home.

"I don't know," she replied. "Edgar says there's a bad flu going around."

"Really? I hadn't heard that," I said. Since when was Edgar Love an expert about flu epidemics?

"You don't know everything, Jessica Walsh," she snapped, then swiftly apologized. "I'm sorry. I don't know what's wrong. Maybe I'm coming down with something myself."

"That's probably it," I said. There had to be some rational explanation for my best friend's behavior.

"I'm out of my perfume," Eva said. "Do you want to come to The Look of Love with me?"

"Okay," I said reluctantly. If that was the only way I could spend time with my best friend, I supposed it would have to do.

On the walk down Main Street, I confided to her how I felt about Dominic. "I've never been jealous before," I said.

"You never had any reason to be," Eva pointed out.

"What do you mean?"

"I mean that you always get what you want. Things come easily to you."

My best friend made me sound like an awful person. "Is that who you think I am? A spoiled brat who gets everything handed to me?"

"That's not what I meant," she protested.

I narrowed my eyes at her. "What did you mean?"

"You've certainly never crushed on someone as much as Dominic."

"I've had crushes before," I said.

"Not like this," she replied. "Now you have something to lose and you're wigging out a little."

"You make me sound crazed," I finally said. I laughed, a little nervously.

She smiled at me and her dimples flashed. "No, I like it," she said breezily. "It's nice that you show it sometimes."

"We've been spending way too much time talking about me," I said. "What's new with you and Edgar?"

"Things are going very well, indeed," she replied.

"That's great." She gave me a sharp look to let me know my bland tone wasn't fooling her. She knew I didn't like Edgar.

"I just need to get some new perfume, and then things will be perfect," Eva said.

"What's that have to do with —" I started, but Eva cut me off.

"Hey, there's Jaci," she said. "What is she doing?"

I looked to where Eva had pointed. Jaci was standing still in the middle of a busy sidewalk.

"It looks like she's sniffing the air," I said.

"Let's go talk to her," Eva said. "I think something's wrong with her."

As we approached Jaci, she growled. "Hey, Jaci," Eva called out to her.

Jaci growled again and then galloped off, but not before I noticed she had been eyeing Eva like the last rib at a barbecue. I also noticed she was drenched in that same perfume that Eva wore.

"Do you think we should follow her?" I asked.

"She'll be okay," Eva said, but she didn't sound like she believed it, either.

"Do you know her mom's number?"

Eva nodded and whipped out her cell phone.

"Voice mail," she said.

"Jaci's long gone, anyway," I said. "That girl is fast."

I stared in the direction Jaci had gone.

Eva tugged on my arm. "C'mon, I need to stop by The Look of Love."

When we walked in, the bell above the door tinkled, but no one came to greet us. It looked like the store was empty, but we could hear raised voices coming from the back room.

"And I told you I'm not going to do it!" Edgar's voice carried clearly through the heavy velvet curtain.

His mother's words were equally distinct. "You'll do it or else."

Eva and I looked at each other and started to inch toward the door, but another customer came in behind us and the bell above the door tinkled again. This time they must have heard it as the argument ceased abruptly.

Ms. Love hurried out. She had pasted a fake smile on her face, but I could tell she was upset about something. Her hands were shaking.

"How may I help you?" she asked.

"Uh, they were here before me," a boy's voice said. It sounded familiar and when I turned around, I saw Wolfgang Paxton. My day was getting better and better.

Ms. Love's smile faltered. "How can I help you?"

"Do you have any more of the special perfume?" Eva asked eagerly.

Ms. Love's smile reappeared. "I'm afraid a new batch won't be available to the general public for a few more days," she said.

"Oh," Eva said. "Not even for a special friend of Edgar's?"

Ms. Love leaned forward conspiratorially. "My dear, the fragrance is extremely expensive. I'm not one to discourage a customer, but are you sure you can afford it?"

"I need that perfume," Eva said stubbornly. "I have all my baby-sitting money saved up. I can afford it."

My jaw dropped. She had been saving up for a trip to a monster museum for over six months. Her parents had promised to take her, as long as she saved half of the money for the trip.

Ms. Love shrugged. "I'll see what I can do." She went to the back room.

"Eva, what about your trip?" I reminded her.

But she wasn't focused on me. She'd zeroed in on the velvet curtains, waiting like a statue for Ms. Love to return.

After making us wait for at least twenty minutes, Ms. Love came back with a raven bottle with a gleaming silver beak.

Eva practically yanked it out of her hands, but Ms. Love only smiled and named a price that made me gasp.

Eva handed over the money without question.

Wolfgang was right behind me, so close that I could feel his breath on my neck. I stuck my elbow out and it connected with his rib cage. "Do you mind?"

"May I help you?" Ms. Love said.

"I'd like a bottle of that perfume," he said. "For my girlfriend." Eva had lost interest in hanging around now that she had what she wanted. She didn't even want to wait for Edgar to come out of the back room, but I was intrigued.

Ms. Love seemed to be considering it. "And who is your girlfriend?"

"Claudia Dracul," Wolfgang said proudly. I didn't really understand what she saw in Wolfgang.

Ms. Love paled. "No, no," she said. "I'm afraid we're all out of the perfume."

"But you just sold her a bottle," he said. He pointed to Eva, who clutched the purple bag to her chest tightly.

"We are sold out," Ms. Love said.

"But it's a birthday present," he said. He looked like he might cry.

For a minute, I felt sorry for him, but then the same old spoiled Wolfgang appeared.

"Give me that," he told Eva. "I'll pay you double."

"No!" she cried.

He reached for his wallet and took out a bunch of hundreds and waved them in her face. "Triple."

"No way," she said. "I'm not selling my perfume to you for any amount of money. Let's go, Jessica."

I glanced at Ms. Love. She was watching the exchange with a carefully neutral expression, but I caught a gleam of satisfaction in her eyes.

Eva was already out the door, so I followed her and dismissed the incident from my mind. I was more worried about Jaci than my best friend's new obsession.

Suddenly, something occurred to me.

"Eva," I said. "Do you have that old bottle of perfume?"

She stopped and stared at me. "Why?" she asked.

"I just . . . like the bottle," I lied.

Eva reached into her purse and handed me the old bottle. Just as I hoped, there was a single drop left in it.

As Eva busied herself dabbing the new perfume on her wrists and neck, I opened the bottle and took a whiff. I was curious to see if it still smelled like dirt as it had when I first smelled it on the day of the grand opening. It smelled like regular old perfume, nothing special, like spices, vanilla, and citrus, but there was a hint of something earthy in there, too.

"It's nice," I said. Lame, but what was I supposed to say? That it reminded me a little bit of wet dirt?

"Nice? That's it?"

"What's the problem?" I said. "I can't afford it, anyway."

"True," she said. "I didn't really like it that much when I first got it, either. But now I just can't seem to get enough."

Eva gave me a wave as she took the turn that led toward her house. I watched her receding figure and felt like she was slipping away from me. It was part of high school, I knew. People changed. I never thought my best friend would be one of those people, though.

I pondered my problem all the way home. There was a car in the drive at the Giordanos, so I rang their doorbell. Rose answered on the first ring, almost like she'd been waiting for me.

"Jessica, come in!" she said. "What's up?"

"I've got a problem I'm hoping you'll be able to help me with," I said. "You're a science major at UC Nightshade, right?"

Rose nodded.

"Have you ever heard of a perfume making people . . . sick?" I asked.

"Like an allergy?" she asked.

"It might be more than that," I said. I pulled out the bottle I'd gotten from Eva. "There's only a drop left."

Rose took it and held it up to see. "That should be enough to analyze it," she said.

"That would be great," I said. "My best friend has been acting really strange ever since she started wearing it."

"I'll take it to the lab tomorrow," she said. "I'll call you as soon as I know anything."

After I left the Giordanos, I went home and took a shower. I scrubbed every inch of my body over and over. The smell of the strange perfume seemed to have leaked into my pores, but I finally felt clean again.

CHAPTER EIGHTEEN

Eva wasn't in school the next day, so I sat with Raven and Andy at lunch and told them about what had happened at The Look of Love.

"Zombies," Andy pronounced through a mouth full of tacos.

Raven rolled her eyes when Andy wasn't looking.

"Zombies? That's your explanation?" I asked.

Andy shrugged. "It's possible."

"I'm so sick of hearing that word," I said. "If it were zombies, wouldn't there be a more widespread outbreak by now? Why do Edgar's Lovelies seem to be the only ones affected?"

"Have you ever even seen a zombie?" Raven asked.

Andy raised an eyebrow. "Fought one. Killed one," she said succinctly.

"You killed someone?" Raven was horrified.

"It was trying to eat me," Andy said defensively. "It's not like I had a lot of choice."

"*It* used to be a human," Raven said.

"Look, newbie," Andy said. "Don't lecture me about how to fight. You don't have the faintest idea what it's like out there."

Raven glanced around to see if anyone was listening, but the rest of the school seemed focused on their food. "For your information, I'm a pacifist," she said.

"How can you be a virago, which by definition means you're a warrior woman, *and* a pacifist?" I wondered out loud. "Not that I'm taking sides," I added hastily, after I got a glare from Raven.

"I will not harm another living being," Raven said stubbornly.

"What about in practice?" Andy said. "You clocked me a good one the other day." She reached over and casually helped herself to Raven's fries.

"That's different," Raven said. "We were practicing defensive maneuvers."

"Does Flo know?" I asked. "And if not, can you warn us before you tell her? I don't want to be anywhere near her when she finds out."

"She already knows," Raven said.

Andy spit out a mouthful of the milk she'd been drinking. "No way!"

"Andy, gross!" I said. I had raised my arms to block

the liquid from getting all over me. "Didn't your mom teach you any manners?"

By the look on her face, somehow I'd managed to put my foot in my mouth.

Without a word, she took her tray and left the table. I stared after her. "What did I say?" I asked Raven.

"Didn't you know?" Raven replied. "Andy's mom died a long time ago. She's an only child. It's just her and her dad. And he works all the time."

"I didn't know," I said. I'd been spending all that time with Raven and Andy and I didn't know something as major as this?

"Maybe I am as self-centered as Eva accused me of being," I said. "I can't believe I didn't know that."

"Don't beat yourself up over it," Raven said. "She never mentioned it to us. I happened to overhear Flo and Andy talking, or I wouldn't have known, either."

The lunch bell rang and I went to my next class, but I kept thinking of the look on Andy's face when I mentioned her mom. I had to find a way to make it up to her somehow.

That evening, I told my mom I was meeting Raven at the Nightshade City Library to do some research. We did have a big project for History. I also wanted to look up witches and zombies, so I decided not to tell her every-thing I was researching.

"Research only," Mom said sternly. "I don't want you using that time to play computer games or update your Facebook status." Like I had time for social networking these days. I could just see my status: *Battling a zombie horde, then lunch @ Slim's.*

She dropped me off at the library, which was packed. There were a bunch of my classmates there, probably try-ing to get a jump on homework, too.

I spotted Ramona, Raven, and Shannon, who were partners for the history project, and went to sit with them.

"Who do you think Edgar will ask out first?" Shan-non asked Ramona. "You or me?"

"Or maybe all of the above." Ramona giggled.

Raven and I exchanged glances. It was obvious they were enjoying their gossip session, but we needed to get some work done.

Raven and I left them whispering at our table and headed for the stacks. "It looks like we're going to have to do all the research," she whispered as she pointed back at our table. Shannon and Ramona were busy dabbing per-fume on their wrists.

I shrugged. "It's not like them to be so flaky. I'm sure they'll pull their weight when the time comes." But I wasn't really that sure.

Raven and I went our separate ways and I found the books I was looking for. I added *Sorcery in Secret* to my stack of books to check out. I was absorbed in a newer book called *Nightshade Through the Ages* when someone came up behind me. I was so startled that I dropped the book on my foot.

I hopped around on one foot. "Ouch!"

"It's me, Jessica," Dominic said. "I didn't mean to scare you."

"You almost gave me a heart attack," I replied.

"Sorry," he apologized again. "Let me take a look at your foot."

"It hurts," I whined.

"It's probably bruised," he said. "Maybe you should stay off it for a while."

"Not going to happen," I said. I picked up the book on sorcery and tried to hide it from him. I wasn't ready to tell him my suspicions about Selena yet. Besides, if I did, he'd probably tell her what I said. Even though he had asked for my help, most of the time he acted like a love zombie.

I was being pretty ridiculous. Selena wouldn't create a zombie outbreak just to get a boyfriend. Would she?

"You're busy," Dominic said. The hurt in his voice pulled me out of my reverie. "I'd better let you get back to it."

I watched him leave and then sighed. What was I going to do about Dominic Gray?

"Trouble in paradise?" Edgar's oily voice interrupted my train of thought.

"None of your business." I tried to leave, but he blocked my way.

"Going somewhere?"

"Get out of my way, Edgar," I said. "What do you think you're trying to do?"

"Trying to change your mind about me," he said. He put an arm up and leaned on the wall behind me.

"Don't bother," I said. "I'm leaving. My friends are waiting for me."

"They left five minutes ago, when you were occupied," he replied. "We're all alone." He stepped closer to me, but I ducked under his arm and ran out of the library.

I was surprised to see Eva outside in the parking lot, looking in one of the big windows of the library, so I ran out to meet her.

"I have to tell you something," I said.

"I saw what you did," she replied accusingly.

My jaw dropped. "What I did?"

"Flirting with him like that." Her voice started to rise. "I thought you were my friend." She grabbed my arm and gripped it tightly.

"Eva, what's wrong with you?" I said. She was squeezing my arm so hard that I was sure to have bruises in the morning. I broke her grip, but it wasn't easy. Where was my alleged super virago strength when I needed it?

"Nothing's wrong with me," she said. "Leave Edgar alone."

"With pleasure," I replied. "He's a creep."

"Ha!" she said. "You were all over him in the library."

"Listen here, Eva Harris," I said. "I'm only going to say this once. He was all over *me*, not the other way around."

She glared at me. "Of course the only guy who has ever paid attention to me *has* to be interested in you, not me. After all, you're Jessica Walsh."

My mouth hung open in surprise before I gathered myself enough to ask, "Where were you today, anyway?"

"I was sick," she said, but I could tell she didn't even believe her own lie.

"Eva Harris, you haven't missed a day of school since I've known you, until now. You've been missing a lot."

"Okay, but you can't tell a soul," she said. "Promise?"

This wasn't going to be good. "Promise."

"I spent the day with Edgar." Her eyes were red-rimmed and puffy.

"You what?" The thought made my skin crawl.

"We hung out at the store," she continued.

"What exactly did you do all day?"

"Get your mind out of the gutter, Walsh," she said. "His mom was there, too."

"His mom knew you were skipping?" I asked.

She nodded. "He showed me his ant farm. He's so cool."

"Ant farm?" That didn't sound that cool to me. It sounded creepy, but I didn't like things that crawled.

Eva didn't pick up on my unease. "It's not one of those little kiddie farms," she said. "It's enormous and they produce this special fungi."

"That's interesting," I replied. I was just trying to be polite, but an ant farm made me want to yawn. "You guys have science together, right? Maybe you can use the fungi stuff somehow for your project." School had barely started before the teachers had assigned semester-long, major-part-of-our-grade type projects in every class.

She clapped her hand over her mouth. "I promised him I wouldn't say anything about the fungi."

She was so nervous about it that I finally felt a trace of interest. Why was Edgar being so secretive about such a harmless hobby? I assumed it was because he would get grief if word got out.

"It's forgotten," I told her. Then I noticed Edgar glaring at us from the other side of the library window. "Now, about the topic. What do you think of doing our project on the history of Nightshade?"

What was with my best friend? We'd had fights before, but never over a guy.

CHAPTER NINETEEN

Eva and I made up the next day, when she was back in school, after I told her I was sorry about a hundred times. But she had some conditions. "I want you to have lunch with Edgar and me today," she said.

"I told you I wasn't interested in him," I said. "Don't you believe me?"

"I believe you," she said. "I don't know what I was thinking. But you also said he was a creep. I want my best friend and my boyfriend to be friends."

Boyfriend? I thought of Ramona and Shannon's conversation in the library yesterday. Edgar didn't seem to be interested exclusively in Eva. But I knew better than to say the thought aloud.

At lunch, I found Eva at a table with Edgar and the other Love groupies. She was sitting on his knee and his arms were wrapped around her. There was a strangely blank look on her face. Was she pretending not to see me or was she just wrapped up in Edgar?

Either way, my best friend was acting like a brainless idiot.

I hesitated, unsure what to do, but then Edgar spotted me and waved me over.

While we ate, Edgar and I were both on our best behavior, but we were both faking it. I was doing it for Eva, but I wasn't sure why he was pretending.

"So Eva tells me you have an ant farm," I finally said, after searching for a neutral topic.

"It's a formicarium, or, for the uninitiated, an ant terrarium," he said.

"Isn't that just another way of saying ant farm?"

Edgar didn't look too happy at my comment and Eva kicked me hard under the table.

"I mean, I don't really know much about the subject, so you could definitely describe me as uninitiated." From the look on his face, he *wanted* to describe me as *stupid*.

He droned on about ant habitats for the rest of the lunch period. Eva and the other girls hung on his every word. I spotted Raven and Andy across the room and rolled my eyes.

In Biology class, Raven leaned over and asked, "What was the deal with you today at lunch? You looked like someone was making you eat sour lemons."

"Worse," I said. "I was forced to talk to Edgar for an entire hour."

"Why?" she asked.

Raven always cut to the heart of the matter. "To make Eva happy, of course. She wants me to like him because she likes him."

"But he's loathsome," she replied.

I shrugged. I was still hoping Rose's analysis of the perfume might explain some things, so I was eager to get home. But first, I had to endure a special assembly that afternoon.

"What's the assembly all about?" Raven asked me as we made our way to the gym.

"It's supposed to be a BMX team," I replied.

High school seating could be tricky. I looked around and tried to find the best place to sit. Claudia and Wolfgang were making out in a dark corner, but none of the teachers seemed to be paying attention to them.

Selena Silvertongue was in the front row with Eva and the other Lovelies. They all wore identical large sunglasses. Eva sat next to Edgar, with Selena on his other side, so I didn't even try to sit by her. Andy waved to us, but she was sitting with a bunch of other juniors, including Bethany and Tiffany.

"Want to find somewhere else to sit?" I asked. "I can only take Eva's sister in small doses."

"There's an empty spot over there," she said.

The curtains were closed, and we sat there for several minutes, but nothing happened. Dominic rushed in and scanned the crowd. Raven and I waved to him and gestured to the empty seat next to me, but his gaze skipped over us until he found who he was looking for.

I swallowed hard when I saw him join Selena and Eva in the front row.

Raven followed my gaze. "It doesn't mean anything," she said softly. "He probably didn't want to climb through all those people to get to us."

But he should, I thought. If he really liked me, he would want to climb a thousand bleachers just to see me.

Principal Amador strode onstage and went to the microphone. "Unfortunately, our guests had an emergency and are unable to be here."

There was a chorus of groans from the crowd.

"Now, settle down," the principal said. "We were lucky that a local celebrity was able to fill in at the last minute. Please give a big Nightshade High welcome to Circe Silvertongue."

The curtains opened to reveal Circe Silvertongue standing in front of a stage kitchen. Her assistant scurried around, stirring pots and pans, while Circe checked her makeup in a large ornate mirror suspended from the ceiling, kind of like a giant disco ball.

"Oh, no," I groaned. "Anybody but her."

The rest of the school seemed thrilled with the idea of free afternoon snacks, but I remembered the nasty taste in my mouth and how she'd set off the fire alarm during the television show taping.

But this cooking demonstration went off without a hitch.

"I'd like a volunteer from the audience, please. Anyone?" Only a few people raised their hands, including Dominic.

Raven nudged me and I nudged her back.

"You, there. The young man in the black T-shirt," Circe said. She pointed straight at Dominic, just as I had known she would.

Dominic jogged up to the stage.

"Since I specialize in cooking romantic dinners for two, I'd like a female volunteer now," Circe continued.

The female half of the student body raised their hands in unison, but Circe picked Selena. Of course.

The assistant carried out a small table and then came back with two chairs, a white tablecloth, candles, and silverware. She transformed the little space with a red velvet divider.

Circe instructed Selena and Dominic to take a seat while she whipped up their meal.

The assistant was joined by Eva and two other Lovelies. They grabbed the familiar silver trays and started passing out snacks.

"I have prepared more than sufficient for the high school," Circe said. "There will be enough for everyone."

When the tray came our way, I took the item gingerly. "It looks harmless enough," I said. "Just a little mozzarella and tomato on toast. How bad can it be?"

But Raven was frozen, her food halfway to her mouth. "I can't believe him," she muttered.

I followed her gaze. Dominic was feeding Selena the same appetizer that lay in the palm of my hand.

"So much for his not being interested in her," I said. Dominic was confirming their relationship in front of the whole school. My fist closed around it and smashed it flat. Juice from the crushed tomato spurted all over my pale blue top and stained it.

"Great, just great!" I said. "I'm leaving."

"There's still forty-five minutes left," Raven said. "You'll get into trouble."

"I don't care," I said. I glanced at the stage again. Dominic was refilling Selena's water glass and she looked in his eyes adoringly.

I left the gymnasium and decided to go somewhere to calm down. I needed a quiet place to hide, so I slipped into the nearest bathroom and stared in the mirror. Then I felt a familiar tingle on my arm, right before complete chaos erupted.

I raced back to the gym, only to be stymied by the flood of shrieking students fleeing the scene.

"What's going on?" I asked.

"Run!" was the reply.

I finally managed to reach the double doors. Principal Amador was onstage, up to his knees in writhing snakes. "Stay calm, everyone! Exit single file. Remember your emergency preparedness drills."

There were snakes everywhere. Of every color and size. I repressed a shudder as I waded through them to get to my fellow viragos.

Raven and Andy were standing on the top bleachers with Dominic. There was a large python wrapped around Selena's waist. Her face looked purple. The others tried to get the snake to release her, but weren't having any luck.

I ran up and grabbed one end of the snake. "Take the other end!" I shouted. "Hurry, there's not much time." Dominic joined me on my end while Raven and Andy took the other end and we slowly managed to force the snake off of Selena. We threw it and it slithered away, probably in search of easier prey.

"Did Eva get out?" I asked Raven.

She nodded, too winded to speak.

"Selena, what about your aunt and her assistant?" I asked, then I realized she'd nearly had the life squeezed out of her. "Just shake your head yes or no. Did they make it out?"

She nodded.

"Let's go, then," I said.

The principal had managed to clear the gym, except for a few stragglers in front of us. Raven and I carried Selena while Andy grabbed Principal Amador and dragged him with us, then shut and locked the double doors behind us.

There was already an ambulance out front, so we carried Selena there and left her in the crew's capable hands.

The principal hustled the rest of us to the designated emergency location and started roll call. Eva, Edgar, and the Lovelies huddled together, but I noticed Edgar's usual smirk had vanished. He looked scared, which was new for him.

Parents were pulling up to the school, and a couple of guys started tossing a football around. Everything looked normal on the surface, except it wasn't.

Principal Amador managed to check off names from some sort of master list and determine that everyone was present and accounted for.

I was happy to hear that. I didn't relish the idea of going back into the gym for a search-and-rescue mission.

"What the heck happened?" I asked.

"Circe was cooking the main course," Raven said. "And then suddenly, snakes started coming out of the pots and pans, out of the oven, everywhere. It was gross."

"It was magic," Andy said importantly. "Someone used magic to get that many snakes into the school."

"No duh, Andy," I snapped. "What are we going to do about them?"

"How are we supposed to find out who did it?" Raven said.

"Did anything odd happen before the snakes appeared?" I asked.

"Nothing," Andy said.

"There was one thing," Raven said. "Claudia Dracul and Wolfgang got up and walked out in the middle of the show. They didn't even try to hide it, either. It was almost like they wanted Circe to notice."

"Not that she would," Andy said. "She was too busy laying into that poor assistant of hers."

Flo arrived on the scene as we debated what to do. Her tattoo must have alerted her to the danger.

"We need to reverse the spell," she said. "It's not anything I can do. I'll call Natalie."

"Natalie?" I said. "How can she help?"

"Natalie is a witch," Flo replied. "Didn't you know?"

Slim's fiancée was a witch? There was so much about Nightshade I didn't know.

Nobody wanted to go back into the school, so the entire student body stood around talking. Dominic finally broke away from his aunt and came back over to our little group.

"Weird, huh?" he said.

Natalie and Slim showed up about five minutes after Flo called them.

"You stay here," Flo ordered. "Natalie and I are going into the gym. We'll call you if we need any assistance."

They were back relatively quickly. "The snakes were already gone," Natalie reported. "Along with every trace of the magic."

"Why didn't Circe use magic to get rid of the snakes?" I asked. "She's supposed to be a super-powerful sorceress after all. And her niece was in dire straits."

I glanced over to where Circe still stood. I couldn't hear what she was saying, but I could tell from her body language that she was berating her poor assistant.

Surprisingly enough, although the assistant kept a meek expression on her face, there was a gleam of amusement in her eyes.

"Jessica, I was so worried about you." Mom came hurrying up. "Are you ready to go home?"

"I'm not sure if it's okay for us to leave yet," I replied. "Let me go check."

Principal Amador gave me the okay, but made Mom sign me out.

She grilled me about the incident all the way home, but I didn't have any answers. Something weird was going on, but I didn't know who was doing it or why.

CHAPTER TWENTY

Poppy, Sarah, and I were in the family room, watching TV right before bedtime. Poppy worked as she watched, stuffing envelopes or some other equally glamorous administrative task for Mom's business.

"I could help you with that," I offered.

"No, it's okay," Poppy said. "I like it. It's kind of soothing. And besides, I can always speed it up if I get behind." Her power was telekinesis, the ability to move objects with her mind. I wondered if Mom knew she'd hired the world's best multitasker.

Circe's latest food disaster came on the local news. They made it sound like a few of the "exotic delicacies" Circe had been planning to serve had escaped. There was no mention of a giant python trying to squeeze the life out of Selena and I knew there wouldn't be.

"I can't believe they don't have a clue," I muttered, but Poppy heard me.

"You mean about what really went down at the gym," she said.

"What did you hear?" I asked her.

"Giant snakes tried to eat Principal Amador," she said succinctly. "Is it true?"

"Pretty much covers it, except it wasn't the principal, it was Selena Silvertongue," I said.

"Why would anybody want to hurt Selena?" Sarah asked.

"That, my dear sister, is the question," I told her. "I'm not sure if it was Selena or Circe they were trying to get to."

"Can you think of anybody who hates Circe?" I asked her.

"Pretty much everybody in Nightshade," Poppy said.

It was true, which meant it wouldn't be easy to find out who was behind sabotaging Circe's television show.

"It's been fun, but I should probably go," Poppy said. "I've got a date with Liam tonight." It was almost ten, but her boyfriend was a vampire. They kept odd hours sometimes.

After she left, our phone rang and my heart jumped, but then reason set in. If Dominic was going to call me, he'd call my cell, not the house line. I picked it up and heard an automated message telling me that school would resume as scheduled in the morning.

All anybody could talk about the next day was the snake attack. I was relieved when the day ended.

Dominic was waiting for me at my locker. "Want a ride home?" he asked.

I hesitated, but I had found out something about sorcery that could explain his attraction to Selena, and I needed to tell him about it. "Sure, if you don't mind waiting. I need to talk to Eva first," I told Dominic, as I spotted Eva in the hallway.

"I don't mind at all," he said.

"Eva, wait up!" I called, but she ducked down a corridor, almost as if she was trying to avoid me.

I followed her. "We're going to talk about this, whether you want to or not."

"Leave me alone, Jessica," she shouted.

"There's no way I'm leaving without talking to you," I replied.

We'd reached a dead end. There was nowhere else to go except the teacher's lounge, and there was no way she'd go in there.

Instead, she snarled at me and then stopped to sniff the air. "What smells so good?" she asked.

"I don't know," I told her. "Maybe you smell Food

and Nutrition class. Raven said they were making brownies this week."

There was a strange look in her eyes. "No, it's not the brownies. It's you."

My tattoo started to tingle and that's when I knew I was in danger. I turned around to face whatever was coming my way. I never suspected the attack would come from my best friend — not until her arms locked tight around my throat.

Her teeth scraped the top of my scalp. "Hungry," she moaned.

I tried to break her hold, but she suddenly had super strength.

I stamped on her foot and put my elbow into her eye. Her eye immediately started to swell, but that didn't stop her. I was losing oxygen, so I reached around behind me and grabbed her arms. I flipped her over my head and threw her to the floor. The impact stunned her.

I bent over, gasping for breath, but she recovered quickly. She was up again, teeth bared. A long string of drool dripped from her mouth. She didn't look anything like the friend I loved.

She tried to punch me, but I blocked her. That's when she bit me. My scream of pain brought Mr. Bennington, the Food and Nutrition teacher, into the hallway.

He took one look at my blood dripping onto the floor

and the crazy look in Eva's eyes. "Principal Amador's office, now!" he snapped.

"But she . . ." I started to tell him what happened, but his glare stopped me. I had planned to go through my entire high school experience without visiting Principal Amador's office.

I stayed behind Eva, where I could see her, and we all three made the long walk down the hall.

"Wait for me here," Mr. Bennington said and then knocked on the principal's door.

"Hungry, hungry, hungry," Eva shouted.

I handed her a banana, left over from my lunch. "Shut up or we're going to get into even more trouble than we already are."

A shudder went through her, and a minute later, she said, "What happened?"

I shot her a dirty look. "Quit faking it!"

"What are you talking about?" Eva looked around. "What are we doing in the principal's office?"

"You've got to be kidding me," I said.

The office door opened. "Jessica, Eva, Principal Amador would like to see you now."

Eva had what looked like a genuinely confused look on her face. What was going on with her?

I couldn't lie to Mr. Amador, but I could limit the information he was given. It was obvious that Eva didn't remember a thing, and who knew what the principal would do if I confessed that my best friend had been trying to eat my brains. Avoidance was the only way to go.

"Have a seat," Principal Amador said. "Tell me what happened."

"What did Mr. Bennington tell you?" I asked.

"I don't understand why we're here," Eva said.

Principal Amador replied, suddenly stern, "You're here because you were caught fighting in the hall."

"Why can't I remember anything?" Eva continued to talk to herself like Principal Amador wasn't even there. I kicked her when I didn't think he was looking.

He was. He raised an eyebrow but didn't say anything.

"It's not what it looked like," I finally said.

"Are you telling me that you and Eva were not brawling?"

Eva answered for me. "Jessica and I are best friends," she said. "We never fight."

"That's true," I said.

"How do you explain how Jessica received that bite mark?"

"I don't remember," Eva said. Tears welled up in her eyes. When she reached up to wipe them away, I saw something that made my stomach churn. A telltale flash of red on her palms. The sign of a zombie.

"Eva wasn't feeling well," I said. "She said she was

hungry and then she just fell on me. Her mouth just kind of hit me."

I was a horrible liar and I could see in his eyes that he didn't believe me, but it was the best I could do in a pinch. "My best friend is a zombie" wasn't going to cut it.

"Hmm," he said. "You may go."

"That's it?" I asked.

"Miss Walsh, what else would you like me to do? There is something strange going on, but since you tell me that it was an accident and it does look like your injury is little more than a scratch, the matter is over. Unless you would like me to call your parents?"

"No, no, that won't be necessary. Thank you," I said, and then hustled Eva out of there before she could say anything else.

I spotted Bethany at her locker and took Eva by the arm and led her there. "Bethany, Eva's not feeling very well," I said. "Could you drive her home?"

Bethany took one look at her sister and said, "What the heck happened?"

"She's not feeling well," I repeated. I wondered if I should tell Bethany the truth about what had happened. I decided I shouldn't, not unless I wanted to be laughed out of school.

"Not my problem," she said. She started to walk away, but I gripped her arm tight and held on. "Look, Bethany, for once in your selfish life, be a good sister and take care of Eva."

"You think you're so hot, now that you're dating Dominic Gray," she said. "I'm not taking orders from you."

It would serve Bethany right if Eva sucked out her brains. I didn't really care what happened to Bethany, but Eva would never forgive herself for eating her sister.

Fortunately, Dominic chose that moment to arrive on the scene.

"Everything all right, Jessica?" he asked. He gave me a quick hug and Bethany glared at me behind his back and stomped off.

"I think I should take Eva to Flo," I said. "Something is wrong." In a low voice, I briefly explained what had really occurred.

"I'll help you get Eva to the car and then find Raven so we can leave," he said.

Eva was docile, obediently following us to Dominic's car. She still had a curiously blank look in her eyes. I sat in the back seat with her. There was no way I was turning my back on her, just in case she got a hankering for brain tacos. Besides, she was my best friend. I grabbed her hand to comfort her, but it was cold and clammy. A minute later, her teeth started to chatter.

On the way, my phone rang. It was an unfamiliar number, but I picked it up. "Hello?"

"Jessica, it's Rose. I have the results of the perfume analysis back."

"What did you find out?"

"The fragrance's base is an extremely rare fungi," Rose told me. "The carrier produces the fungus and then spreads it by getting others to absorb it through their skin or eat it."

"The carrier? How can I tell who or what that is?"

"Probably an insect of some kind," she said. "But that's not the weird part."

"What's the weird part?"

"The fungus causes symptoms similar to zombie-ism. It's crucial that we isolate the carrier before we have an outbreak on our hands."

"I think it's too late," I said with a sob. "I think we already have a zombie outbreak on our hands. And my best friend is one of the victims."

CHAPTER TWENTY-ONE

"Bring Eva to Slim's," Rose said. "I'll meet you there. And hurry. We might not have much time."

Dominic came back with Raven in tow and we took off for the diner.

Rose met us at the door. "Get Eva to drink this," she said.

"What's in it?" I asked.

"Just get her to drink it," she ordered. "It's the best I could do on such short notice."

I reached out to take it from her and she noticed the bite mark on my hand. She grabbed my wrist. "Hold still," she said. "What happened?"

"Eva bit me," I said. The mark had turned a strange purple and my hand was swollen.

Eva sat down obediently while Raven fed her Rose's concoction.

Flo frowned at me. "You might have mentioned that before now." She wheeled around and stomped to the office.

"What did I do wrong?" I wondered.

"It's just Flo being Flo," a voice said. "Sit down and rest." I looked around but couldn't figure out where the voice came from.

I started to feel woozy. I swayed, but Dominic grabbed me and steadied me. He helped me to a booth. "What's wrong with me?" I asked. "I feel hot."

Flo came back, but she didn't look happy. I'd probably flunked some virago test I didn't even know about by getting bitten by the first zombie I met.

"It's the virus entering your bloodstream," Rose said matter-of-factly. "Here, drink this."

"Virus?"

She gave me a look. "Jessica, concentrate. Remember what I just told you on the phone about the zombie fungus?"

"Z-zombie . . . me?" I asked.

She nodded. "Now drink up."

I took a cautious sip. "It tastes like feet," I complained.

"Drink it," Rose repeated. "Unless you want to get a sudden craving for brains."

"Gross," I said. I shuddered but drank every drop without further protest.

The place where Eva had bitten me felt hot and itchy.

"Stop scratching it," Raven said. "Remember what Rose told you."

"It itches like crazy," I told her.

Rose put a hand to my forehead. "You're hot," she said, frowning. "Someone needs to watch them overnight."

"We can do it," Dominic said.

"What will we tell our parents?"

"That's easy," Raven replied. "We'll have a slumber party at my house. My aunt's a nurse, so she can help if—"

"What if I get the munchies for human flesh?" I said. The thought repulsed me.

"You won't," Dominic said. He squeezed my hand.

"I hope the antidote will start working and kill the virus before it gets to that point," she said.

"What about Eva?"

Rose's silence said it all.

"There's got to be something we can do!" I said. "She's my best friend."

"There may be something," a voice said from somewhere. Everything seemed far away.

"You mean a cure for Eva?"

"If you can find the source, you may have a chance to find a permanent cure," Slim told me. "Rose was able to fix up something for you because you'd only recently been infected. But for Eva to have those cravings, she must have been infected long ago. That concoction will only slow her progress, it won't stop it. Not until we find out how she caught it."

My thoughts were jumbled. In the background "Rolling in the Deep," by Adele, was playing on the jukebox. An idea occurred to me. "Dominic, what were the songs you sang? You know, when you were predicting in song? I think those songs were clues."

I grabbed a paper napkin and borrowed a pen from Flo. "What was the first song? 'Crazy for You,' right?"

Dominic blushed. "I think that one may have been personal," he said.

I must have looked confused, because he leaned in and whispered, "That was the night we met, remember?"

"Oh." Now I was the one blushing.

He ticked off the rest of the list and we all examined it.

"'Ant Music,'" Andy pointed out. "Didn't Eva tell you that Edgar Love has an ant farm?"

"But what about 'Love Potion Number Nine'?" Raven asked. "Or is that another personal message, too?" She nudged her brother.

"Oh, my god," I said. "*Love* potion. It's Edgar Love. Or his mom. They've been using their perfume to turn people into zombies. Eva got a special bottle of perfume from The Look of Love."

"Anybody else?" Flo asked.

I nodded. "A bunch of girls got the perfume bottles, which was a raven with a silver beak."

Flo looked worried. "There could be a lot of infected girls out there, then."

"I don't think they made very many bottles," I finally said. "But I know who they gave them to."

"Do you think you can find Eva's?" Slim asked. There was a thread of tension in his voice that told me we were almost out of time.

Raven was already rummaging through Eva's purse. "It's not in here," she said.

"I'll find it," I said. "I have to. It's probably in her bedroom." I would do almost anything to save my best friend.

"You don't think her mom has noticed that there's something wrong?" Dominic asked.

"Probably," I admitted. "They've always been close. But I can't tell her the truth."

"We're running out of options," Flo said.

Natalie said, "If you can get your hands on a bottle of that perfume, between my magic skills and Rose's science expertise, we should be able to create an antidote."

"Dominic and Raven, you go with her," Flo ordered. "Just in case."

Five minutes later, they hustled me to the car and we

were on our way to Eva's house. Raven sat in the back seat with me, just in case I tried to eat the driver.

Raven walked with me to the door while Dominic waited in the car.

My head was throbbing and I thought I was going to throw up, but I thought of Eva and managed to avoid hurling all over her front porch.

Mrs. Harris answered the door. She had the same bright brown eyes and dark hair as Eva. "Why, hello, Jessica. Eva's not here right now."

"I know," I said. "I came over to ask if . . . if," I felt myself sway, but Raven wrapped an arm around me and smiled at Mrs. Harris, while she tried to prevent me from slumping to the floor.

"We wanted to know if Eva could spend the night at my house," Raven said. "My aunt will be there and we're going to rent movies."

"I would like to talk to your aunt first, but other than that, I don't see any problem," Mrs. Harris replied.

"Eva asked us to pick up her PJs and stuff, if that's okay," I managed to say. "She's off with Nurse Phillips, picking out the movies."

Mrs. Harris smiled at me. "You know what that means, don't you?" she said. "Nothing but werewolves and zombies.

I tried not to flinch when she said zombies.

"You girls go ahead," she continued. "You know the way, Jessica."

"This is interesting décor," Raven commented.

Eva's room was lime green and purple, but I knew it was the mess Raven was talking about.

"We'll never find anything in here," she said, staring at a mound of clothes in the corner.

"Believe it or not, Eva has a system," I told her.

"Not," Raven said.

I pointed to a pile closest to her dresser. "That's the newest stuff. Let's check it. The perfume is either there or in her bathroom."

We went through the pile very carefully, but I didn't find the black bottle with the silver beak.

"Nothing," I said.

"Me, neither," Raven said, and she sat back on her haunches and looked around the room. "Does Eva have a hidey-hole or anything?"

"She hides her diary from Bethany," I said.

"I can see why," Raven said wryly. "Do you know where it is?"

"Ted Vicious!" I had already crossed to the enormous teddy bear that Eva had "redesigned" a few years ago. She'd carefully cut a hole in Ted Vicious and created a hiding place. She then pierced his ears and gave him a Mohawk and a patch over one eye.

Her diary was gone, but in its place was the bottle we had been searching for. I held it up to the light. "There's still a good amount left."

"Hopefully, it'll be enough," Raven said.

"Let's go," I said.

"Wait a minute," Raven replied. "We told Eva's mom we were getting her stuff for a sleepover."

"Thanks for the reminder," I said. "I need to call my mom."

Mom okayed the slumber party at Raven's. "I have training the next morning," I added. "And then we're going to get something to eat. I might not be home until late." Luckily, I'd never skipped curfew or given my mom anything to worry about, so she agreed readily.

I was feeling better, but my thought process would suddenly go dark and I couldn't think. "I hope Flo's remedy starts working soon. My brain is all fuzzy."

We grabbed Eva's overnight bag, said good night to Mrs. Harris, and headed to the car, where Dominic was singing along to the radio.

He looked so cute sitting there that I suddenly wished that I wouldn't turn zombie, not before he kissed me, anyway. Of course, that wasn't likely to happen now, not when he knew I might nibble off his lips.

We cruised by the diner and I carried the perfume bottle very gingerly inside. I didn't relax until I'd put the perfume into Natalie's hands.

"I'm so glad you found it," she said. "I'll get to work on the antidote."

Eva was curled up in a booth. "How is she?" I asked Flo.

"A little better, I think," she said. "But you need to keep a close eye on her."

Dominic and Raven and I hauled Eva out to the car.

I'd never been to Nurse Phillips's house, but it wasn't what I expected. It was a cute little one-story bungalow with a swing on the front porch. The living room was painted pale green and there was a lemon-colored couch practically covered in floral pillows.

Raven seemed to read my mind as I looked around. "It's not very rocker chick, is it?" she commented. "Aunt Katrina really loves flowers."

We walked down the hall to her room, which was decorated, in stark contrast to the rest of the house, in reds, blacks, and whites. There were no posters or photos on the wall, with the exception of a photo of a much younger Dominic and Raven with two adults, who I assumed were their parents. The woman in the photo looked just like Raven.

"Is that your mom?" I asked.

Raven didn't look at the photo. "Yes," she said shortly.

I sat Eva down on the bed and took off her shoes before helping her into some jammy pants and an old *Dawn of the Dead* T-shirt. She was glassy-eyed and feverish, but at least she didn't try to take a chunk out of me.

She did, however, have screaming nightmares. Worst sleepover ever.

Around midnight, there was a tap at the door. "Everybody decent?" Dom asked through the door.

"C'mon in," I said. "It's not like anyone is sleeping, anyway."

He came in carrying a guitar. "I thought maybe a song would calm her down." He sat on the floor by the bed and strummed gently on the guitar.

He played her a lullaby I recognized from my childhood. Eva recognized it, too, because she snuggled back down in the bed and fell fast asleep.

"Thanks," I said softly. "I love that song. My mom used to sing it to me."

"Mine did, too," he said. He stood. "It's getting late. I'd better let you get to sleep yourself."

After he left, I watched Eva's sleeping face. I had to figure out what was going on. I couldn't let my best friend turn into a zombie.

The next morning, Eva's mom arrived early at Nurse Phillips's house, to pick Eva up.

We tried to stall her. "We were going to make waffles and then do our nails," I said desperately.

Eva was glassy-eyed and nonresponsive. "Eva," her mom scolded her gently. "I can tell you were up half the night. I bet you girls didn't sleep a wink."

"You have no idea," Raven muttered quietly.

"We're going to visit my aunt in San Carlos," Mrs. Harris said. "She's in the hospital."

I let out a long unconvincing sneeze. "I think I'm coming down with something," I said in a nasally voice.

I nudged Raven and she caught on quickly. "Me, too."

"Gee, I hope Eva hasn't caught it," I said. "She was up sneezing and coughing half the night."

Mrs. Harris frowned. "My aunt is still weak," she said. "Maybe it's best if Eva stays here. I wouldn't want her to spread any germs at the hospital."

That bought us a few hours.

After Mrs. Harris left, Raven asked, "How are you feeling, Jessica?"

"I think Flo's nasty-tasting stuff actually worked," I said. "I wish I'd known what was really going on with Eva. I would have force-fed her a gallon of it weeks ago."

"Tired," Eva said.

She looked terrible. "Maybe more sleep would do her good," I said. "I'll take her back to your room."

Raven nodded. "Maybe you should try to take a nap, too."

"I don't think I'll be able to," I said.

I led a docile Eva back to Raven's room and tucked her in before climbing into the other bed.

I must have fallen asleep, because the afternoon sun streamed through the window.

I yawned and stretched and then checked out the other bed. Eva was a small lump under the covers.

My stomach growled and I realized I was starving. "Eva, wake up," I said. "Time to rise and shine." I reached over to give her shoulder a shake, but my hand met pillows instead.

"Eva!" I called, then called for her again. But she was gone.

CHAPTER TWENTY-TWO

My best friend had disappeared, and although we spent the rest of the day looking for her, we didn't spot her anywhere. We finally gave up and everyone went home. I hoped that Mrs. Harris stayed at the hospital a long time.

I couldn't stand just sitting around waiting to hear what had happened to Eva, though, so I decided to go for a run. A nice long jog would give me time to think and work on conditioning at the same time.

It was already dark, but I knew Nightshade like the back of my hand. I ran so long that I lost track of time, but finally stopped when I got a stitch in my side.

I was near the park, where I could take a shortcut home. Although I usually avoided the park at night, it was getting late and my mom would be worried.

I walked at a brisk pace. There were a lot of missing-pet signs up, but I attributed it to coyotes, or maybe a peckish vampire.

I was in the middle of the park when my tattoo started to burn. I looked around, but I didn't see anyone. Still, it made me nervous and I broke into a slow jog.

Flo's order to never go anywhere alone repeated over and over in my brain and I wanted to kick myself for being so stupid. The only thing to do now was to get out of the park and to somewhere public as soon as possible.

The burning sensation continued and I heard footsteps behind me.

I started to run and heard someone running behind me. I told myself that it was just a random jogger.

Then I felt a tight grip on my arm. I wheeled around and took a fighting stance, but it was only Shannon.

"Jessica, I've been calling you for five minutes," she said. "Are you okay?"

"J-just a little nervous," I said. My heart rate started to slow at the sight of a familiar face. It dawned on me that Shannon was one of the Lovelies and a big fan of perfume. My tattoo burned even more than before.

"It's not safe for you to be out here all alone," she said. "There's no one here to hear you scream."

Her grip on my arm tightened.

"Shannon, are you all right?" But I already knew the answer. She smelled like sweat and dirt. She'd been infected. I tried to break loose, but she was drawing me closer.

I tried to remember Flo's tutorial about zombies. You couldn't reason with them because their brains were being flooded with chemicals telling them that they were hungry for one thing. Human flesh.

Shannon was taller and outweighed me by a few pounds, but I had my virago strength and the element of surprise.

She propelled me toward her and I used the movement to topple her to the ground. She let go of my arm and I took off running.

As I ran, I noticed other eyes gleaming in the darkness and then the sound of several people — at least I thought they were still people — running after me. I glanced back. A mob of hungry-looking zombies were chasing me. I spotted more of my soccer teammates and a girl I sat next to in Spanish class, but the zombie leading the pack was Eva. So much for our Best Friends Forever necklaces.

I ran faster than I'd ever run in my life. I ran until I hit Main Street. There were no other people on the street and I could feel the zombie girls gaining on me. I spotted the diner sign and made a break for it.

I burst into Slim's. "We have a big problem," I said to Flo, who was sitting on her favorite stool at the counter. Andy and Raven were sitting next to her. "I'm being followed by a horde of zombies."

Flo got up and calmly locked the door. "Tell me what happened." I noticed her T-shirt, which read PLEASE DON'T FEED THE ZOMBIES.

I related the encounter, then said, "You've got to finish that antidote, fast!"

A tap on the door made me jump, but it was just Dominic and Selena.

Flo let them in. I glared at Dominic. I was sick of his game playing.

"What are you doing here?" I asked.

"Selena has something to tell you," Dominic said.

"I'm not interested!" I snapped. "I have bigger things to worry about right now than Selena."

"You're just jealous!" Raven said.

"Your best friend isn't the one who is infected," I said.

Raven clapped a hand over her mouth. "Jessica, I didn't mean it. It just slipped out."

I got up and walked through the kitchen to the back door, ignoring their pleas to wait, to let them explain, to whatever.

I made it outside before Slim stopped me.

"That is a very stupid idea," he chided. "And you do not strike me as stupid."

I snorted.

Slim tried another tactic. "If you get eaten, Selena will

have Dominic all to herself, so please don't go out that door."

I didn't turn around, but I heard him leave. He made a lot of noise, probably to reassure me that he was going to let me make my own decision. I stayed there for a few minutes, feeling like an utter fool.

Slim was right. Walking out in a huff was bad enough, but I would have gone straight into the arms of a zombie mob.

I'd let my temper get the best of me again. If I were really honest, I'd admit it wasn't anger that motivated my almost exit, it was jealousy.

I walked slowly back into the main part of the diner.

But when I returned to the diner, Selena and Dominic were sitting in a booth, their heads close together. I started to inch back out of the diner, but Dominic looked up and saw me.

"Jessica, I'm glad you're back," he said. "We have something to tell you."

My heart dropped to my stomach. I'd finally been convinced that I'd been imagining there was something between them, but now I was going to have to hear my suspicions confirmed, after all.

"Yes?"

"Why don't you sit down?" Dominic said.

"I'd rather stand," I said curtly.

He grabbed my hand and tugged me down next to him. "I know you're mad at me, but just listen to what Selena has to say, please?"

I nodded, completely mystified.

Selena cleared her throat. "I have a confession to make," she said. "Dominic's not in love with me. I used my powers to convince him he was."

"Why would you use magic to get a guy to fall in love with you? You're gorgeous. You could have any guy at school."

"Any guy except Dominic," she replied. "I've promised never to do it again, to him or anyone else. He's forgiven me."

"And the cooking show sabotage? Was that you?"

She gasped. "I'd never do anything like that."

I gave a skeptical snort. "We know two things about who sent the snakes," I said. "Whoever it was has magical powers. And they hate your aunt, Selena."

"Who do you know who fits that description?" Dominic asked gently.

"You can't mean me. I would never do anything like that. I love my aunt." Selena's lip trembled. "In fact, that's what I wanted to talk to you about. Aunt Circe has lost her magical powers. She's too ashamed to admit it. But after the snakes invaded the school . . . It's getting too risky for me to cover for her anymore."

I thought for a minute, back to the research I had done on sorcery when I was trying to help Dominic. "I read somewhere that powers can be siphoned off," I said. "Is there anybody you can think of who might do that? Anyone with a grudge against your aunt?"

She raised an eyebrow. "Not many people like my aunt," she said. "I know that."

"What happens if her show gets canceled?" Dominic asked. "Does anyone on the show stand to gain from its cancellation?"

She shook her head. "Everyone would lose their jobs."

A thought occurred to me. "What about your aunt's assistant? I think her name is Brooke."

Selena gave me a puzzled frown. "Brooke wouldn't hurt a fly. She's an unpaid intern."

"Your aunt is kind of tough on her," Dominic said. "And if she's an unpaid intern, she won't care about losing her job."

"What about someone closer to your aunt?" I said. "She recently married Count Dracul. How did his grandchildren feel about that?"

Her silence said it all.

"We have another problem to deal with right now," I said. "But thanks for telling me. I'll keep my eyes open."

She stood. "Thanks, Jessica. I'll see you later." I watched Dominic's face as she walked away, but he didn't seem to be fixating on her.

"Selena, be careful out there," I called after her.

Dominic and I sat there, not saying anything.

Rose and Natalie emerged from the kitchen, where they'd been working tirelessly.

"We've got some bad news," Natalie said.

Rose sighed. "There's just not enough of the fungus in the perfume sample we have to create enough antidote for all of the infected girls. I'll try something else, but I can't make any promises."

Andy looked determined. "Then we're just going to have to go straight to the source and collect more fungus."

"Let's go," Flo said. "We'll split up. Jessica, you and Raven go to the store, and Andy and I will head for the Loves' house."

"I'm coming with you," Dominic said.

But when we left Slim's, he suddenly took off at a jog. "I just thought of something," he said. "I'll meet you there."

Raven called out, "Where are you going?"

But he was already out of hearing and didn't respond.

"He'll be all right," Raven said. "He knows how to take care of himself."

"The Look of Love. What a joke," I said.

CHAPTER TWENTY-THREE

When we reached the store, it was closed. I pressed my face against the window, but everything was in darkness.

Raven knocked loudly on the front door, but there wasn't any answer. "Nobody's here," Raven commented.

"Let's try the back," I suggested.

I spotted Eva slipping through the back door and grabbed Raven and pulled her behind a Dumpster.

Eva didn't hesitate, and just went through the back door.

My tattoo began to throb. "I'll bet you money that the rest of the Lovelies will be right behind her."

Shannon was the next one to arrive, followed by Jaci, and then Ramona.

Raven peeked around the Dumpster and leaned so far out that she almost fell. "Don't let them see you," I hissed.

We waited almost an hour, but no one else went in or came out. Raven was practicing tai chi in the corner.

"I'm going in there," I said. I'd lost my patience.

"I think we should wait for Flo," she said.

"I'm sick of waiting," I replied, and went straight in the back door of The Look of Love. I didn't wait to see if she followed me or not.

The door, as I expected, led straight into the storeroom. But the room was empty and there was nothing particularly ominous about it. It was a plain old storeroom with perfume bottles and boxes and a mini-fridge beneath a bare lightbulb. The Loves' pet raven was nowhere in sight.

"Where did everybody go?" I muttered.

"Let's see if they're in the front," Raven replied.

I gave her a grateful look. I was glad to have some company, even if it was a virago pacifist who would be of no use to me in a fight.

The store was completely empty.

"Where are they?" I was frustrated.

"Maybe we missed them leaving?" Raven suggested.

"There's no way," I said. "I've been staring at that door for the last hour."

We wandered all around the store without spotting any clues.

"I guess we should leave," I said. "We've found out exactly a big fat zero."

We headed back through the velvet curtain. The back room was in darkness. I didn't remember switching off the light.

Raven was in front of me when I heard a dry cough and then a thud.

"Raven? Are you okay?" I knew something was terribly wrong when my foot hit something solidly fleshy.

I edged away from the solid form and tried to get to the light switch. I heard someone behind me, another raspy breath. I whirled around ready to fight, but before I could connect, someone gave me a big shove and then I was falling. I slid for a long time, down some sort of chute, and then landed with a thud.

I groaned and then stood shakily and tried to get my bearings. A sticky substance trickled down my throbbing leg. I must have cut it on something.

It was pitch-black, but when I put out my hand, I could feel rough edges of a wall. I put out the other hand, but didn't touch an opposite surface.

I couldn't reach a ceiling, either, and imagined that I looked something like a mime trapped in an invisible box, if anyone could see me in the darkness.

My heart rate sped up.

"I'm not trapped," I said aloud. "I'm just momentarily stuck." I reached for my cell phone, but it wasn't in my pocket. It must have fallen out when I tumbled down the rabbit hole.

I willed myself not to panic. The first thing I needed to do was find a way out. I was pretty sure I was underground. The earth was damp to the touch and there was a moldy smell in the air, dank and rotten. I went deeper into the tunnel, groping the wall and walking slowly in order not to do any more damage to myself.

There was a faint light in the distance and I moved a little faster. Maybe it was a way out. Maybe Raven had realized what had happened to me. Maybe it was help.

It was none of these things. As I got closer, the tunnel widened into a large cavern.

The light came from several camping lanterns, which were propped up along the walls of what turned out to be a rather large anthill. And I was facing a rather large ant. I don't mean the kind that crawls up your arm and you notice that it's an inch bigger than all the other ants.

This ant was so big that it took up nearly all the cavern, which was of considerable size. The front half of her was a bright red and there were tall spiky tendrils coming out of her head.

And the Lovelies, who were standing next to the creature, were seemingly oblivious to the fact that a monster-size insect was currently making them look about the size of real ants.

It didn't take a genius to figure out who was behind the giant ant in the basement. Edgar had taken his love of ant farms just a tad too far.

He and his mother sat at a card table in the back of the cavern. It looked like they were using the cavern as extra storage for the store as well as a place to do evil deeds.

Edgar gripped Raven's arm tightly, but she stood there passively. So help would not be arriving in the nick of time, and it was up to me to save us.

I moved closer and Raven's eyes lit up. She'd obviously spotted me. I put a finger to my lips and ducked behind a cardboard cutout of Edgar and the Lovelies.

"What were you thinking?" Ms. Love asked. "You brought two viragos down here, you idiot." She whacked Edgar on the head.

"They were snooping around," he said. "What did you want me to do?"

She didn't answer his question, but continued to scold. "Your obsession with that ant is what got us into this mess."

"You said I needed a hobby," he said.

"There's no help for it," Ms. Love said. "I'll have to fix your screwup. Again. Where's the other virago?"

"If we're lucky, the queen already ate her," Edgar muttered.

"Witnesses?" his mother asked sharply.

"Just the Lovelies," Edgar said. "And we both know *they* won't be any problem."

They both laughed.

Ms. Love tapped her chin and thought for a second. "We'll have to get rid of your pet, I'm afraid."

"But you promised. You said I could have a pet, as long as I produced the fungus for your perfume," he replied. He sounded like a pouty five-year-old.

"You can have one of the Lovelies or the queen, but not both," his mother said.

"But —" Edgar started to protest, but his mother cut him off.

"Decide quickly. We still have to harvest the fungi and make our exit."

"I like it here," Edgar said stubbornly.

His mother's coddling tone turned cold and deadly. "Then, perhaps you should reconsider your complete inability to make an intelligent decision. Find the other virago and dispose of them both."

"Yes, Mother," Edgar replied. "How should I get rid of them?"

"Must I think of everything?" she asked. "Feed them to the queen."

Edgar twisted Raven's arm, hard. "Tell me where she is."

"I thought you said the ant got her," Raven said.

He twisted harder. "The queen is still hungry, which means your friend is still alive. Now tell me where she is."

I stepped out from my hiding place. "I'm right here," I said. "Come and get me."

My tattoo started to tingle so much that it felt like a burn. I wheeled around and came face-to-face with half of my soccer team, who, unfortunately, eyed me like I was on the menu.

"I'm so tired of people trying to eat me," I said. I had no choice. I was going to have to go all Fight Club around my friends.

I threw Shannon over my shoulder and spun her around and used her legs to knock Eva and Jaci down.

I thought the battle was over, but then I felt an arm wrap around my neck and start to squeeze. Edgar.

Raven hit Edgar with a fold-up chair. He went down and stayed down.

"Thanks," I croaked.

"What about Ms. Love?" Raven asked.

Edgar's mom was gone, but we had bigger problems.

"What is that thing?" I asked.

"Thing? *Thing?*" Edgar was conscious again and practically turned purple with anger, which was funny, if you thought about it. His face would match his cheesy T-shirts.

"The queen is hungry," Edgar snapped. "Feed her."

I barely had time to wonder what was on the menu before Shannon and Eva each wrapped an arm around me and propelled me toward the enormous ant.

I came face-to-face with Raven, who had Jaci and Ramona flanking her. They lined us up and then pushed us closer to the ant's mouth.

The queen's mandibles reached for us, but it didn't seem like she was really that hungry. More like she'd already eaten a huge meal but would take the last cookie on the tray just because it was there.

Raven's eyes went wide with fright and she struggled to free herself from her captors. She managed to wriggle loose and then she ran from sight. I stared after her, stunned. My fellow virago had deserted me when I needed her most. I knew she was a pacifist, but that was taking things a little too far.

The queen was disinclined to chase after her food. Instead, she turned her attention to me. Without warning, her giant pinchers snapped an inch from my face. My long red hair was probably the equivalent of waving a red flag at a bull. I didn't want to test that theory.

When she didn't manage to grab me, she spewed

something noxious, but I ducked just in time. It sprayed all over Shannon.

I nearly gagged when I looked up and saw Shannon licking the stuff off her hands with every appearance of enjoyment. Eva joined her and licked the stuff off Shannon's arm like it was an ice cream cone. Ramona scooped some off the ground and ate big handfuls.

I used their momentary distraction to break free, but then Jaci ran toward me. I thought she was going to tackle me, but instead she joined her friends in a fungus feast.

I spotted a door directly behind the queen ant, but she wasn't going to let me simply waltz on through. I looked around, but there wasn't anything I could use as a weapon.

Queenie lunged at me again and I jumped out of the way. Suddenly, she was more motivated to eat me. She attacked again and her huge mandible caught me a glancing blow and knocked me to the ground.

I was lying there, stunned and out of breath, trying to figure out my next move, when she charged again. What worked on a monster-size ant?

A lantern, probably dropped by one of the Lovelies in her haste to chow down on the disgusting fungus, lay on the ground just out of my reach. I rolled over and grabbed it and held it up in front of the ant, but it barely seemed to register with her.

She was quick, but I was quicker as I rolled again, away from her, and then onto my feet. My only hope was to run for that door. I hated to leave Eva, but I didn't have any other choice.

I ran, faster than I'd ever run before, with the queen behind me and gaining on me. I made it to the door, but to my horror, it wouldn't budge.

I spotted a metal curtain rod and grabbed it, just as the queen pinned me to the ground. I dropped the curtain rod.

A large drop of slime from the ant's jaws hung an inch away, and as I turned my head from the stench, I saw the rod, just out of reach. I stretched my left arm and grabbed it.

Ms. Love picked that moment to reappear, directly between the queen and me. She ran at me, fist raised, but I grabbed her arm and bent it back until she grimaced with pain.

"Don't hurt her!" Edgar screamed. I wasn't sure if he was talking about his pet or his mom.

I shoved his mom straight into his pet's jaws. There was a loud scream and I looked away.

When I looked back again, Ms. Love was gone. There

was a pool of blood seeping into the dirt and next to it was a single finger. I bent over and threw up.

My stomach was finally empty and I glanced over my shoulder to see the mutant ant bearing down on me again. The queen was still hungry. As the ant's jaws descended, I hit her with the curtain rod with all my might.

There was a shriek of pain and then a rain of noxious red spores.

I wiggled away from her body before it collapsed on me, and then tried not to throw up again. The ant's head had exploded.

I took the stairs two at a time. I needed to get help, just in case something had happened to Raven. I didn't want to think about what that something might be.

CHAPTER TWENTY-FOUR

At the top of the stairs, I could hear footsteps. Help had arrived! But when I opened the door, it was Raven.

"Let's get out of here," she said. "We'll lock them in the closet until we figure out what to do with them."

We dragged Edgar into the closet first and then made repeat trips to round up the Lovelies. We left Eva for last.

"I hate to leave her in there with him," I said.

"It's not like we have any other choice," Raven replied.

"I know," I said. "It's just, she's my best friend, you know?"

"I know," Raven said. "But how do you think Eva would feel if we let her bite someone else?"

"Help me move her."

"Let's hurry!" Raven said. "Before Ms. Love gets back."

"I don't think she's coming back," I replied. She looked puzzled but didn't ask any questions.

After they were all tucked inside the closet, it was a tight fit. We put a chair under the door handle.

"We'd better check in with Flo," Raven said. "She's probably frantic."

Raven hung up her cell. "Flo says they're on their way. But we should leave the building. Just in case they get out of the closet."

We were outside when Andy, Dominic, and Flo arrived a few minutes later. "Where are the girls?" Flo asked.

"Locked in the closet with Edgar," Raven answered.

"Are you okay?" Dominic asked his sister. "No injuries?"

"I'm fine," she said. "Quit fussing."

"Jessica, you call Rose and tell her we have enough fungus for an antidote," Flo ordered.

I reached in my jacket, but then I remembered. "I lost it in the cavern," I said.

"Here, use mine." Raven held her phone out to me but wouldn't meet my eyes.

I took it from her reluctantly. She'd choked under pressure, and I didn't want to have anything to do with her at the moment. Viragos needed to be able to count on each other. I couldn't figure out if she'd run because she was scared or because she was a pacifist, but either way, that wasn't the reaction I wanted from a fellow virago.

I gave Rose the news and she told me that she and Natalie were on their way to the store.

"We need to get Edgar out of that closet before they eat him," Flo said.

"It would serve him right," I replied.

"We need answers," Flo snapped. "And Edgar is the only one around to give them to us."

We trooped back inside the store and I showed her where we'd stowed the Lovelies and Edgar. She opened the closet door and dragged Edgar out by his collar.

Flo sat him in the office chair. "Talk," she ordered, but Edgar crossed his arms and remained irritatingly silent.

I was stymied. Why would Edgar want to turn a bunch of girls into zombies in the first place?

"Why did you do it?"

"I needed workers to take care of the queen," he said. "The fungus made it so the girls were . . . obedient."

"You turned girls into zombies because you needed help taking care of your pet?" I wanted to slug him, but instead I settled for hurting his feelings. "The queen is dead," I told him bluntly.

A single tear rolled down Edgar's face.

"What's the cure?" I demanded, but he just shrugged in response.

"You're going to let all those girls remain in that

state?" I asked. "I can't believe that even you are that low."

But apparently he was. He refused to say anything else and no amount of begging and pleading worked. So we tried threats, bribes, but he still wouldn't answer one more question.

"I'm tempted to shove him back in there with them," I said. Low moans came from the closet. I hated to think of Eva slowly disappearing and leaving just a flesh-hungry shell, but if we didn't do something fast, that's what would happen.

"We'll just have to figure it out without him," Flo said. "Hopefully the antidote will work."

Natalie, Rose, and Slim arrived.

Slim asked me about the whereabouts of Ms. Love.

"She could be down there in that enormous ant farm," I said. "But I shoved her in front of the queen. I didn't see what happened to her. Then I killed the ant queen."

"We'll take care of it," Flo said, and she headed down to the basement with Slim. To my surprise, Rose and Natalie didn't need the fungus we harvested. They already had an antidote ready. They took vials of the cure into the closet where the Lovelies were trapped.

I paced up and down until they returned. "Did you find a body?" I asked. "I didn't see whether or not the ant got her."

"Yes," Flo said. "At least part of one — a finger. The acting police chief is checking prints now, but we're pretty sure it belonged to Ms. Love."

After an agonizing amount of time, Natalie and Rose emerged from the closet.

"Did it work?" I asked.

Dominic took my hand while we waited to hear Rose's response.

"I won't know for a few hours."

"How did you figure out the antidote?" I asked.

Rose replied, "Dominic was a big help."

"Dominic?"

"He managed to find another bottle of the perfume," Rose said.

"Where did you get it?"

"Selena," he said. "That's where I went."

"Just to get the perfume," he added, after a quick look at my face. "I remembered that she had mentioned Edgar had given her some, but she hadn't bothered to open it yet."

Rose continued. "I knew it was a fungus in the perfume, and I assumed the treatment would be similar to treatment for other fungal infections. Then, with Natalie's help, I made a few adjustments."

"You girls should go on home," Flo said.

"No way," I replied.

"I'm staying, too," Raven said.

Hours passed. I tried not to look at the clock. Rose finally checked on the Lovelies and then came back.

"Did it work?" Raven asked.

"I think so," she replied. "Eva said she wants a double cheeseburger and the rest of the girls seem hungry for real food, too."

"At least no one is requesting brains," Andy commented.

We all had to laugh at that, but it was tired laughter.

CHAPTER TWENTY-FIVE

We were still trying to figure out how to tie up a few loose ends.

"What about the mutant queen?" Raven asked. "What are they going to do with the body?"

We all looked at each other. What could you do with the carcass of a fifty-foot-tall killer queen? There was a long silence.

"Shrinking spell," Natalie finally said. "I'll do a shrinking spell on her."

It seemed like hours before Slim and Natalie came back up the stairs.

"Well?" Flo asked expectantly.

"All done."

"You're sure the spell will hold?" I asked.

Natalie nodded. "I'm sure."

Flo made a quick, quiet phone call, then hung up.

"Slim, why don't you take everyone to the diner and feed them? They must be starving. I'll wait here. I need to update the council."

"What will you tell Mr. Bone?" I asked. Nicholas's dad was the leader of the city council.

"The truth," Flo said.

"The truth?" I stared at her. "Will he believe you?"

"You'd be surprised what he'd believe," she replied, then cracked a smile at my doubtful look. "Jessica, you have a lot to learn about Nightshade."

I guess I did. Strangely enough, I was looking forward to it.

Raven walked ahead with Slim and Natalie, which left Dominic and me to walk side by side. Things were awkward between us, even though he had been worried about me.

I cleared my throat. "I guess I owe you an apology."

"Why?"

"Because I didn't believe you when you said things weren't right between you and Selena."

"You were a little busy trying to save your friend," he said gently.

When we reached the diner, Slim said, "Lunch is on me."

We grabbed a booth and Slim whipped up burgers and fries for all of us.

He'd just served us, when Flo, Andy, and the Lovelies walked in. Shannon, Jaci, and Ramona seemed a little dazed, but otherwise back to normal.

Flo guided them gently into a booth, but Eva walked right up to us on her own.

"I'm so hungry I could eat a horse," she said.

I jumped up. "Eva," I said, "do you remember . . ."

"That I was a zombie? Sure," she said.

I hugged her. "I am so sorry that I didn't figure it out sooner," I said.

"Are you kidding?" she said. "I've always wanted to write my own horror novel and now I have actual experience. It's better than a movie."

"I'm so glad you're back to your old self," I said. "I missed you."

"I missed you, too," she said. Then her attention wandered and I followed her gaze to see who she was looking at.

Evan and a couple of his friends were walking in the front door. He gave us a wave but didn't come over to talk.

Eva's hopeful smile vanished.

"He has a right to be mad at me," she said. "I was mean to him. I completely ignored him. For Edgar." She shuddered. "What's going to happen to them? Ms. Love and Edgar, I mean?"

"Ms. Love either escaped or was eaten," I told her. "I'm hoping for the second one. But Nightshade City Council has Edgar in custody."

Eva sighed and glanced over at Evan again.

"Go talk to him," I urged. "Tell him what happened." His two friends had left the table to feed quarters into the jukebox.

"He'll think I'm insane," she said.

"If he does, then at least you'll know," I told her.

"Know what?" She tilted her head, puzzled.

"That he's not the right guy for you," I said. "He's alone right now. Now go." I gave her a little shove.

It didn't take any more encouragement. She went over and said something. Evan looked up, seemed to be considering something, and then gestured toward the empty seat next to him.

"That was nice what you did," Dominic said.

"She deserves a little happiness after what she's been through," I said.

"So do you," he said.

The moment was interrupted when Natalie came in with Poe on her arm.

"Where did you find him?" Eva cried, jumping up from her seat next to Evan.

"We found him hiding in one of the cupboards," Natalie said. "I think I'll have to take him to the animal shelter. He doesn't like me. I doubt he'll get along with my familiar, either." As evidence, the bird snapped the air, obviously trying to connect with one or more of her body parts.

"Don't do that," Eva said. She jumped up and reached out to pet the bird.

"Careful," Natalie warned. "He bites."

"Oh, Poe is an old softie, isn't he?" Eva cooed. "I'm going to ask my mom if I can keep him."

Leave it to my best friend to have a pet raven.

To my surprise, Wolfgang and Claudia entered the diner, followed by Selena, and then Circe and Count Dracul and Circe's assistant, Brooke.

"The viragos found out who has been sabotaging the television show," Selena explained. "And I wanted Jessica to explain it to you."

I groaned inwardly, but gave everyone a game smile. I'd had bigger things on my mind, such as surviving the weirdest ant infestation ever. The television food disaster mystery had slipped my mind.

"We think that the culprit was someone who didn't like Circe," I said. "But that left a whole lot of suspects."

Count Dracul shot his wife a stern look and she gave

him a guilty smile and a shrug, as if to say, "I am who I am."

He softened and reached over and held her hand.

"But the last stunt was done with intent to harm someone," I said. "At first I suspected Claudia because, let's face it, Circe isn't her idea of a step-grandmama."

Claudia faced me with a level stare and I wondered if it was such a good idea to tick off a vampire. "And she did have access to the high school," I continued. "But she doesn't have any magical abilities and I assumed that if she wanted to get to someone, she would use other methods."

Claudia gave me a long slow smile that sent shivers down my back. "You are correct," she said. "I prefer to deal directly with any . . . issues."

"So that left either Brooke or Wolfgang. And although it seems like something Wolfgang would do, and he's not above having someone do his dirty work, it wasn't him."

All eyes turned to Brooke, whose demeanor went through a quick transformation. Suddenly, the meek little intern was an intimidating sorceress.

Still, I was shocked when she actually admitted it.

She said, "Yes, I did it. So what? There's nothing you can do about it. Because what Circe isn't telling you is that she's somehow managed to lose her magic."

"What? Darling, is this true?" Count Dracul.

She nodded. "Weeks ago," she said. "Selena's been helping me cover."

"Why didn't you tell me?" the Count asked.

"I was embarrassed," Circe replied.

Brooke ignored us all and got up from the booth. "Now, if you'll excuse me," she said. "I have another appointment.

"Not so fast," I said. "You're not going anywhere."

Brooke actually laughed in my face. "And you think you're going to stop me?"

"Nope," I said. "But they will." I pointed to Natalie and Mr. Bone, who grabbed Brooke by the arm and escorted her away.

I turned to Circe and said, "I think you'll find your powers will return in a few days."

"How?" she asked. The hope on her face made me hope I'd guessed correctly.

"I'm pretty sure Brooke has been siphoning off your power to use it against you," I said.

"My power did start waning not long after she became my intern," Circe said. "I can't believe I trusted that imbecile." So much for the kinder, gentler Circe.

"I am indebted to you," the Count said to me. "If there is ever anything you need, please do not hesitate to call me."

"I can't believe it was Brooke," Selena said. "I didn't think she had the nerve."

"Jessica, I want to talk to you about something," Dominic said. "Alone."

There was an uncomfortable feeling in my stomach and my heartbeat quickened. I took a bite of my salad to stall what I was sure would be an awkward conversation. I chewed slowly until my heartbeat returned to normal.

Everyone else in the diner suddenly got extremely busy elsewhere.

"Shoot," I finally said.

"I wanted to explain about my mom," he said. "Raven told me what she said to you."

"About what?" I was lost and it showed on my face.

"How she was surprised that I like you," he said. "It's not about you."

"It's not? Then who could it possibly be about?"

"My mother's not dead," he said flatly.

My mouth fell open and a little piece of salad tumbled out. I snapped my mouth closed and brushed the lettuce out of sight.

"She's not? But you said —"

"I didn't lie," he said. "But I didn't tell you the truth. I just said she's gone. She abandoned us to travel the world, fighting. She's a virago, like you and Raven."

I tried to absorb the information calmly but my mind raced. "That's why Raven said she was surprised you wanted to go out with me." And maybe that's why Raven was trying to be a pacifist.

He nodded. "But a virago has a choice, you know. You don't have to go from city to city. You can decide to be the protector of one place. She chose to leave."

I reached for his hand. "I'm so sorry, Dominic." I couldn't imagine my mom ever leaving us, or my dad, either. In a way, Dominic had lost both of his parents. Just not the way I thought. "Do you ever hear from her?"

"Not very often," he said. "As you can imagine, she was thrilled when she heard that Raven was following in her footsteps. Too bad Raven hates being a virago." We looked across the diner at his sister. "Raven is the most gentle person I've ever known. Can you imagine how hard it is for her to actually fight?"

"I can now," I said softly.

"She's stuck for seven years, and that's after she finishes her training."

"Is it true, though, what they told us? That we have no choice? Maybe there's a way she doesn't have to fight."

"Why would Flo lie? Or my mother?" But there was a trace of hope in his eyes.

"Maybe they're not lying," I said. "Maybe it's just what their trainers told them."

We stared at each other, stunned by the possibilities behind my impulsive words.

"If you had a choice, a real choice, would you want to be a virago?" he asked me.

I didn't know what to say, but I settled for the truth. I met his eyes. "Yes, Dominic, I would." I'd rather never have a boyfriend at all if I couldn't be myself around him.

He nodded. "I'm glad you told me the truth."

"And?" I was waiting for bad news, but it didn't come.

"And what are you doing next Saturday night?" he asked.

"You mean you still want to go out with me, even though I want to be a virago?"

He cupped my face gently. "Jessica, I want to go out with you no matter what."

He was about to kiss me, when there was the sound of loud throat-clearing.

"Sorry to interrupt," Slim said. "But, Jessica, your mom is on the phone and she sounds mad. Something about laundry not getting done."

"Ah, the glamorous life of a virago," I said with a laugh.

My life in Nightshade wasn't exactly glamorous, but no one could say it wasn't interesting. I wouldn't trade it for anything.

Acknowledgments

Thanks to my agent, Stephen Barbara, my editor, Julie Tibbott, and everyone at Houghton Mifflin Harcourt. And thanks to my husband, Michael, who always manages to fix whatever technological gizmos I've managed to break.

Marlene Perez is the author of *The Comeback*, *Love in the Corner Pocket*, and the six books in the Dead Is series, including *Dead Is the New Black*, which was named an ALA Quick Pick for Reluctant Young Adult Readers. She lives in Orange County, California, with her family. She acts like a zombie until her first cup of coffee.

www.marleneperez.com